My Bestfriend's Man

2

P. Dotson

"Are you Savannah Lee?" one of the uniformed officers asked me.

"Yes," I said nodding my head. I could feel myself near tears and I had the slightest idea why they were even there. Roxie pushed her way past them and stood by my side.

"I'm afraid we have some terrible news. There's been an accident."

"Accident?"

"There was a fire?"

"A fire?" I repeated. He was prolonging what he had to tell me. I could see it in his eyes the news wasn't good.

"I'm sorry to tell you this but your parents were killed in a fire."

Savannah

A month has passed and I'm still trying to find a way to deal with it. To escape from the pain I try to stay busy, picking up extra shifts on the job here and there whenever Donna will let me. I need something to keep me occupied or I might just go crazy. Donna keeps telling me at a time like this I need to hold strong to my faith and give all my burdens to the Lord. She says he will never put more on us than we can bear. That's something my mother would say. It's just hard to keep an open mind with the holiday's right around the corner.

I've been attending church a lot more, doing all I can to hold strong and put all my trust in the Lord. It's helping me keep my sanity. I try to attend the prayer meetings, the Friday night service or whatever service they have in general. It helps, but I still have those moments where I just cry and I can't stop. I get so angry sometimes just wondering why. Why me? Why them? I know we're not supposed to question God but I can't help but to wonder why. Why would he take them away from me?

The last you heard my parents were killed in an accidental fire. But an official investigation revealed they were murdered. Whoever killed them tried to cover their tracks by setting the house on fire. Neighbors called the police and the fire department just in time before the house was completely engulfed in flames. I hate to even talk about it. An autopsy revealed both my parents suffered severe blunt force trauma to the head. They suspect it was a burglary gone wrong because items were missing from the house, but I'm not convinced.

I have a good support system around me but I still feel empty inside. I've lost both my parent's and my little sister Gabby who died years ago. Roxie my best friend since grade school has been very supportive but even she can't fill the void that I'm feeling right now.

I clutch my pillow tighter trying to take myself to a happier place but it didn't work. If I could just turn back the hands of time. I tried to stop the tears but they forced their way past my eye lids and slid down my cheeks. I'm tired of crying because no matter how long or hard I cry I know it will never bring them back.

"Savannah," Brian whispered my name as he gently touched my shoulder. I forgot he spent the night with me. I tried to wipe the tears away before he could see them but it was too late. He handed me a tissue and wrapped his arms around my waist. "Its okay baby," he whispered in my ear before placing his nose in my neck.

I grabbed his arm and sunk deeper into his embrace. Brian my current boyfriend has stayed by my side since the beginning. To think I almost ended things with him right before all this happened. We snuggled for a good thirty minutes, without saying a word. He left me to my thoughts, and didn't bombard me with a bunch of questions and I appreciated him for that.

"You want me to fix you some breakfast babe?" he asked kissing me on the forehead. I glanced up at the clock on my stand. It was almost ten o clock in the morning. As much as I wanted to lay around in bed and mope I knew I had to get up.

"Yeah," I sighed, sitting up and nodding my head.

"Okay. Go ahead and run yourself a nice bath or take a hot shower. It might make you feel better," he said. I nodded my head and mouthed okay. "I'll be right back," he said giving me his beautiful smile. As soon as he walked out the door I rolled off the bed and walked into the bathroom.

The water felt good against my skin. I stood in the shower for a good ten minutes wishing some how the water could wash away my pain and take away this emptiness that I felt. I could feel the tears coming on again so I quickly turned the water off. I stepped out, grabbed a towel, and wrapped it around my body. I had a chance to lotion up, throw on some clothes, put my hair in a sloppy bun and Brian still hadn't returned yet. I started to go downstairs and see if he was burning up my damn kitchen but my cell phone began to dance on my stand. I sighed because I'm really not in the mood to talk this morning but I decide to answer it anyway.

I walked over to my stand and picked it up. As soon as my eyes landed on his picture my heart skipped a beat. I glanced back at my bedroom door before looking back down at my cell phone. My palms started sweating and I licked my upper lip as I contemplated on whether or not I should answer. I took to long to decide because my phone stopped vibrating and the only thing on my screen now was a message alerting me of a missed call.

I held the phone in my hand before clutching it to my heart. My ex boyfriend Brandon was the love of my life. I thought he was my forever and a day. He was the beat to my heart, the air I breathed, and the blood that ran through my veins. I swear that nigga gave me life. But every fairy tale doesn't have a happy ending. He cheated on me, not once but twice. Like the saying goes fool me once shame on you fool me twice shame on me. My phone started to vibrate. I glanced down at it. It was him again. I felt like I'd be cheating if I answered. I glanced back at my bedroom door; still no signs of Brian. I quickly slid my finger across the green button.

"Hello," I whispered.

"Savannah." His voice made my heart flutter. For a second my voice got stuck in my throat. "Hello," he said. Finally I released the breath I was holding.

"Yes, I'm here."

"Are you busy?" he asked.

"No, why what's up."

"Nothing, just calling to check on you. I haven't had a chance to talk to you since the funeral. I just figured you needed your space."

I really need you is what I wanted to say but I didn't. "Yeah," I sighed.

"So how have you been?"

"Just taking it one day at a time. I still have my moments but all I can do is give it to God and let him handle the rest."

"I feel you on that," he said followed by a brief pause. "I just feel bad you know," he chuckled a little. "Despite how things went down between us your parents still treated me the same. Whenever I would see them in passing they would always ask when I'm going to stop by and I always promise them that I would. That's one promise I won't get a chance to keep." My parent's loved Brandon. We were together for eight years so they grew on each other. They loved him like he was their own son, especially my mom. I don't think anyone after him would have ever measured up.

"Brandon, you can't beat yourself up about it."

"I know, it's just this has made me realize life is too short to hold onto grudges. We haven't really gotten the chance to sit down and talk properly. We may never get the chance but despite all the bull shit we've gone through this past year just know that I love you Savannah. I always have and I always will."

"I love you too Brandon," I whispered as I quickly wiped away the tear that slid down my cheek.

"If you ever need anything, I mean *anything* please don't hesitate to call."

"Okay," I responded. I knew our conversation was ready to come to an end but I really didn't want it to. Despite all the pain and heartache he caused me my heart still beats for this man.

"I'll see you around then. Don't be a stranger."

"You neither."

"Aight I'll talk to you later."

"See ya," I said never taking the phone from my ear for what seemed like minutes. Brian's voice startled me out of my wishful thoughts and I jumped.

"Breakfast is served," he sang as he walked through my door holding a tray. The smell hit me before he did. I didn't realize how hungry I was until I heard my stomach growl.

"Thank you baby," I said sitting back as he placed the tray over my lap. He kissed me on my forehead. I smiled up at this similar version of Morris Chestnut. He had this look in his eyes and I knew he was about to say the three forbidden words that I had just so effortlessly said to Brandon, but I couldn't find it in my heart to say to him. I quickly grabbed a piece of bacon and practically forced it in his mouth. "Here have some."

"Dang baby," he laughed as he took a step back.

"My bad," I answered as I started stuffing my own face. I stole glances at him as he made his way back around to the other side of the bed. I like Brian a lot and I appreciate all that he has done for me but it wasn't love and I doubt that it will ever be. He sat down beside me with this huge smile on his face. "What are you smiling about?" I asked.

"Well, I have some good news."

"Do tell," I said nodding my head willing him to continue.

"I got an offer on my house. I'm supposed to meet with the buyer today and hopefully we can get things going-,"

"Wait, I didn't know you were selling your house," I said cutting him off. An uneasy feeling settled down in the pit of my stomach.

"I told you a couple days ago," he said. I searched my memory bank, and shook my head no. "It was the day me, you and Roxie chilled over here watching reruns of Charmed."

"I still don't remember."

"Well it doesn't really matter anyway," he said shrugging his shoulders like its no big deal.

"Okay, so are you buying another house or what?"

"No," he smirked like I asked him a stupid question.

"Where are you moving then?" I asked although I wasn't in the mood for the answer or the argument that would follow.

"Here," he said with a slight frown creasing his forehead.

"Where?"

"Here," he said pointing down at the bed but I knew what he meant.

I sighed, shook my head, and looked away. Don't get me wrong I appreciate Brian but this is too much for me to deal with right now. See shit like this is why I almost called it quits with his ass in the first place. He wanted us to move in together before my parents died and I told him I wasn't ready, but here he is practically forcing the issue. He wanted more than I was willing to give him. I'm in mourning not desperate.

"Brian-,"

"What's wrong?" he asked me, as he gently began to rub my hair. I looked at him and suddenly chills ran down my spine. The look in his eyes made my heart skip a beat. "Savannah?"

sighed and swallowed the lump in my throat. I moved my head and pushed his arm away. "Brian, I really don't think that is such a good idea."

"Why not?" he asked looking at me like I was crazy.

"Because I'm just not ready."

"Well, when will you be ready Savannah? Do you know how many women would kill to be in your position right now? I'm a good man and I've stuck by your side since everything went down and you sitting here treating me like I ain't shit."

I snapped my neck back because this negro is seriously tripping. Is he not my man? Isn't that what he's supposed to do? I guess he's looking for a reward for good behavior. I'm being real nice and patient with this man, but my patience is starting to wear thin. If he think he is about to take me on a guilt trip he has another thing coming.

"Are you fucking serious right now, Brian? I'm not treating you like anything. I appreciate your support I really do but if you think this guilt trip you trying to throw on me is going to work it ain't happening. We had this discussion before my parents . . .," my voice trailed off. I took a deep breath and rubbed my temples for a moment. I couldn't bring myself to say it openly. The reality of it was still too painful. I looked at Brian and shook my head. I pushed my tray of food towards him and laid back down. "I think you should leave Brian."

"Savannah," Brian started.

"Hey Vee," Roxie came sauntering through my bedroom door uninvited as usual but damn I'm sure glad to see her.

Saved by the bell, I thought to myself. Although Roxie can be suffocating her presence at this moment is welcomed. Brian and I definitely needed to talk. This is something I can't just sweep under the rug, but I just didn't have the energy to deal with him or his demands right now. He wanted to capitalize on my vulnerable state of mind, but I'm not having it. You better believe I'm checking that ass later. Roxie walked around to my side of the bed and hugged me. I didn't even have to look Brian's way. I could already feel the animosity that circulated the air.

"Hey sis," I said sitting up and giving her a hug. I swung my legs over the side of the bed.

"Savannah, we need to talk," Brian said after a moment of silence.

"How are you holding up hun?" Roxie asked sitting down beside me without acknowledging Brian. I heard him sigh and I ignored his ass just like Roxie.

"Savannah I have to go. We'll talk later," he said as he leaned over and kissed me on the cheek.

"Yep," was my reply. I was in my feelings about the little stunt he tried to pull. He couldn't just invite himself to live with me without my approval. I'm definitely going to have to address that shit.

Roxie sucked her teeth and rolled her eyes as he made his exit. It's no secret that she's not a big fan of Brian's. Well, she wasn't a big fan of my ex boyfriend Brandon either. She has always been protective of me. She's my best friend. We've been friends since grade school. We've had some rough patches over the past couple of months because she is so possessive. I think she had a little crush on me, but I quickly shut those thoughts down. I love Roxie to pieces but more like a sister.

"Vee ," she started, calling me by the pet name she gave me when we were kids ."He is such a lame. You can do so much better than him. I would rather put up with Brandon than his punk ass," Roxie said rolling her eyes.

"Roxie, don't start," I sighed dragging my hands down the side of my face. Brian still had me in my feelings but I wasn't in the mood for man bashing either.

"Aight, I'm just saying," she said smacking her lips.

"So how's life?" I asked ready to change the subject. "Are things still good between you and Prince?"

"I don't know Vee. Its like after the funeral things between us took a left turn. I don't know where we stand right now." I nodded my head as she continued to talk. "You know I'm not the emotional type but I took Mom Karen and Pop Gerald's death hard Vee. I was literally there minutes before it all happened."

The last line she said made my heart skip a beat and my stomach do somersaults. Accusations begin to circle around my head like a whirlpool. I shook my head to relieve the negative thoughts attempting to invade my mind.

"Bum ass Detective Harley hasn't been by my house lately," she said rolling her eyes. "I swear Vee I almost caught a fucking case behind his ass with his sarcastic attitude. He kept asking me the same dumb ass questions. Like where was I the night in question, or if I had anything to do with it," she said with a pained expression on her face.

I could identify with the pain that danced around in her eyes. I felt like shit for even thinking that Roxie could possibly be involved in what happened to my parents. She loved them just as much as I did. My parents took Roxie in and raised her as their own when her parents died in a car accident. She began to sniffle.

"Please, don't cry Roxie," I begged.

"I'm not," she said fanning herself. "I just feel like maybe there was something I could have done. This has me all fucked up," she cried as tears slowly leaked from her eyes. "I was just there, and that's some shit I have to live with for the rest of my life."

"Roxie, it's not your fault," I said moving closer to her. I wrapped my arm around her and she laid her head on my shoulder.

Her actions caused a chain reaction. I found myself crying right along with her. Lord knows I miss my parents. I know that we all have to go someday but this was so unexpected. I wasn't prepared for them to be taken from me like that.

I hated being in the dark about what really happened to them. It made it even harder for me to come to terms with the fact they are really gone. I need answers. I need to know something in order to move on with my life. I know rest won't come easy until I find out who's responsible.

"I'm sorry Vee," Roxie said sitting up and wiping the tears from her eyes.

"It's okay. I think crying is a way of cleansing the soul," I replied wiping away my own tears.

"I guess Vee," she sighed. "This is going to be hard," she said looking up at the ceiling.

"Tell me about it," I added. "No more holiday dinners, no more mother, daughter, or father daughter talks."

"I know. I just try to think of it as they are in a better place now."

"I know Roxie."

"As much as it hurts we can't keep doing this to ourselves Vee. They wouldn't want this." I nodded my head because she was right.

"I've got to get to the bottom of this Roxie. I won't rest until I do."

"We will," she said patting the back of my hand. "Whoever did this won't get away with it, I promise."

I nodded my head although doubt circulated through my body. So far they haven't had any real leads. Roxie was under a heavy cloud of suspicion. At one point she was considered the number one suspect. Detective Harley has never really come out and told me that but his questions always became more aggressive whenever he talked about Roxie.

"I can't wait until this shit comes to the light so I can tell those pig muthafuckas to kiss my ass," Roxie said rolling her eyes as she tossed her hair over her shoulder.

I looked at her and for the first time I felt a twinge of jealousy. She was put together. Her long hair looked like it had been freshly pressed with a part down the middle hanging loosely around her shoulders. She actually had on some decent attire today. She had on a pair of black seven skinny jeans, a white shirt and Michael Kors tennis shoes owned her feet at the moment. A far cry from the usual booty shorts she wore that barely covered her massive ass. Roxie is a beautiful red bone, with stunning green eyes. At times her ugly attitude out shined her beauty. I know I probably look like shit, with this whack ass bun. I know my eyes are probably puffy and swollen from crying.

"Are you okay Vee?" she asked me. I nodded my head yes.

I kind of felt bad for Roxie though. She couldn't even mourn her loss without cops stalking her front door. I understand they are just doing their job but I honestly believe they're barking up the wrong tree. The room grew silent as it appeared we each dived into our own thoughts. For some reason my mind shifted to Brandon. I miss him like crazy. My parent's death only made me think of him more. In a perfect world he would be the one by my side instead of Brian. But like the average man he couldn't seem to keep his dick in his pants. As bad as I want him it will never happen. There's no way I can ever put my trust in him again especially since he had the chick up in my house. I sighed and shook my head.

"Hola mami's."

I looked up and smiled. "Hey Zee." Zaheeda is my co-worker. We both work on the maternity ward as Registered nurses at PRMC hospital located in Salisbury, Maryland. I looked at Roxie who tried to roll her eyes on the sly but I caught it. That's Roxie. I looked from Roxie to Zaheeda. I don't mind the company but I wonder how they even got in my house at this time of morning. And a phone call would have been nice but for now I won't complain. Brian must have left the door unlocked . . . again. I shook my head and sighed.

"What's up with ole dude?" Zaheeda asked giving me a hug before sitting down on the bed beside Roxie.

I frowned. "Who . . . Brian?"

"Yeah, he had a major attitude. He barely opened his mouth to speak to me." I rolled my eyes and sucked my teeth. "Is everything good in wonderland?" Zee questioned raising an eyebrow.

I really wasn't in the mood to discuss me and Brian right now. Zee was well aware of me and Brian's strained relationship. Maybe I'm at fault for allowing things to go this far. I mean I kind of feel bad. I just needed a temporary fix to take my mind off Brandon and Brian happened to be it. I didn't expect for him to up and fall in love with my ass though. What he said earlier was right. A lot of woman would kill to be in my position.

Brian owns his own club and from what I hear it's doing well. He has more than enough money to take care of me and anything my heart desired, but I'm not impressed by his money, his cars or his house. I have my own shit. My parents had nice insurance policies leaving me as the sole beneficiary so with that extra money I really don't want for anything. But I've never been the materialistic type anyway. I'm a sucker for love. Right now there is only one man that still holds my heart and it's not Brian.

"Earth to Savannah," Zee said waving her hand in front of my face.

"I'm still here," I laughed.

"So what's going on with you two now," she asked looking over her shoulder at the breakfast Brian prepared for me. It was still in my bed. It was probably cold by now but that didn't stop her from grabbing a piece of bacon and stuffing it in her mouth.

"Same shit different day, I guess. Things between us were good but he always takes things to another level." I said shaking my head getting a little agitated.

"Hmmmm, he must have made you mad; got you up here cussing."

"Shut-up," I laughed. "But I mean this negro just told me he had a potential buyer for his house."

"What?"

"Yeah. Mind you I didn't even know he was selling his house. He says he told me." Zee curled her lips up. "My thoughts exactly. Anyway so I ask him is he buying another house or where is he moving?"

"What he say?" Roxie asked deciding to jump in on the conversation.

"He had the nerve to say here." I guess Zee thought it was funny because she burst out laughing but I didn't find anything about the situation humorous. I gave her the screw face. "What's the joke because I'm all for shits and giggles."

"The look on your face is priceless," she finally answered. "But, you allow it to happen. You don't want him Savannah, why not just tell him. He gone keep on pushing and pressing buttons until he finally gets what he wants."

"I just feel bad. How do you break up with someone who's pretty much helped me through one of the most traumatic experiences of my life? I can't just walk away. I mean how can I do that?"

"Easy just do it," Zee said with a shrug of the shoulders.

"It's easier said than done."

"Everything is easier said than done, but at the end of the day if you want to keep putting yourself through these unwanted conversations that's on you. I told you what you need to do and what you should have done a long time ago. But it is what it is. You might as well let his ass move up in here."

"Really Zee?" I asked giving her a sideways glance.

"Really," she answered stuffing another piece of bacon in her mouth.

I'm not in the mood to entertain her or her opinions. Who asked her anyway?

Roxie

Ugh I can't stand Fajita . . . Zaheeda whatever the hell her name is. What the hell is a damn Zaheeda anyway? Her mother needs to be slapped for that one. That bitch talking about she got Indian in her blood . . . girl bye. If that's the case she needs to waltz her happy ass back to India. I pushed the pedal to the medal, as I took my aggression out on the congested streets of Salisbury. I stopped by Starbucks and ordered me a Frappe. I needed something to calm my nerves.

Zaheeda is one bitch that gets under my skin. Whenever she comes around she just takes over. All she does is talk, talk, talk and talk some more. I couldn't even give Vee a few words of advice because of her overbearing ass. I wanted to tell Vee that she should leave Brian too if she wasn't happy and that he was being too pushy but no, that fake burrito had to put her two cents into *every* fucking thing.

I drove around for a few to calm myself, and then I carried my ass on home. There's no need in venting about that bitch. There isn't anything I can do about her . . . yet. As I walked into my home and stepped into my living room a sense of loneliness came over me. For some reason I didn't want to be alone tonight. I stepped out of my tennis shoes, retrieved my cell phone from my hip and dialed Prince's number.

Prince is kind of my boyfriend. He's actually Brian's little brother. It rang twice then went straight to voicemail. I took the phone away from my ear and looked at it. I hope he's not ignoring me. I tried to shrug off the notion but I couldn't. Ever since Mom Karen and Pop Gerald's funeral he has been acting funny. I shrugged my shoulders at it. The day is still young so I figured I would get a work out in, but before I could head upstairs to change my clothes a knock came at my door. I frowned as I placed my phone back on my hip.

"Who is it?" I yelled as I headed to the front door.

"Detective James Harley." I stopped dead in my tracks and rolled my eyes.

"Fuck," I said out loud to myself. He's getting on my first, second, and last nerve with his old gay ass. He had to be gay. I'm a bad bitch and even if caramel isn't your flavor you still couldn't help but to want a taste. Not this sorry dough boy here though. He always had this serious face like he was about his business. Please. "Just a minute," I yelled all the while rolling my eyes. I slowly opened my front door. "Can I help you?"

"Can I come in?" he asked.

"No."

He smirked than had the nerve to chuck spit out the corner of his mouth. I cringed with disgust as I looked up at his big burly ass. He probably was a good looking man at one point and time in his life, but I guess years of stress from the job have taken a toll on him. I know he had to be at least six three, with thinning brown hair with gray pieces invading his hair line. His blue eyes were cold as ice, his pale skin looked ragged and tough. His clothes were disheveled and he was in need of a shave. Stale cigarette smoke illuminated from his body insulting my nostrils. As I looked at his pathetic ass it was hard to keep a frown from crossing my face. Is this what our justice system has resorted to? Some washed up he has been too lazy to do his job. I shook my head and folded my arms across my chest. I was ready to get this over with.

"I have a few questions to ask you? Are you sure you don't want to do this inside?"

"It's probably the same questions you asked me the last time and yes outside is fine." He cleared his throat and rubbed his dingy chin. I sucked my teeth.

"So where were you the night in question?"

"What is the night in question?" I asked with an attitude. He smirked again.

"The night of August twenty fifth I believe."

"I already told you this."

"Would you mind refreshing my memory?"

I sighed. "I had to go to the store, but since I was out I figured it would be nice if I stopped by to see Mom Karen and Pop Gerald. I hadn't seen them in a while-,"

"I thought you ran into Ms. Lee at the mall, while you were out with their daughter Savannah?" he asked interrupting me.

"I did, but what does that have to do with anything?"

"I'm just making sure I have all the facts. You said you hadn't seen *them* in awhile, but you just admitted yourself that you saw Karen at the mall. Am I correct?"

The foul odor of his breath occupied the space between us. I turned my nose up at the sour smell he let off and my eyes seem to have a mind of their own because they sure did get lost in the back of my head. I could feel my heart beating against my chest like a drum. My armpits were starting to sweat and my leg started jumping.

"Everything okay?" he asked. I guess he could sense that I was a little nervous. I can't understand why though, because I'm innocent for once.

"Yeah, I just don't feel good," I said wiping the sweat off my forehead. I had to get it together and fast. This is not like me, I never fold under pressure. "Can we do this another time?" He looked me up and down and chucked spit out the side of his mouth again. He was being disrespectful, but I held my cool. He fished around in his pocket.

"Here's my card."

"I already have one," I replied as I took a step back.

"I'll be in touch Roxie," he smirked at me then had the nerve to wink.

"Why the hell do you keep harassing me? I didn't do anything?" I snapped. He stood there with a smirk on his face. He looked from his right then to his left and scratched his head.

"You don't remember me do you?" I shook my head no. "Let's go back . . . say thirteen years. You remember a little girl by the name of Gabrielle Lee?" I swallowed the lump in my throat. I could feel my heart rate speed up.

"Yeah I remember Gabby, Savannah's little sister. What the hell does she have to do with this?" I snapped. I was two seconds from slamming the door in his face. He stood there like he had all the pieces of this puzzle put together. The look he gave me, gave me chills.

"It has a lot to do with this . . . because you killed her."

*****

I was glad when Detective Harley decided to carry his filthy ass home. He had me in my feelings and I was a nervous wreck. I wonder what the fuck he knew. The suspense was killing me and had me feeling some type of way. I really don't want to be left alone with my thoughts so I call Prince again. He answered this time, but his ass claimed he was busy. Bri was at work and Savannah said she wanted to be by herself tonight. I could have called one of my Johns but more than likely that would require sex and I just wasn't in the mood. Detective Harley had my mind fucked up.

Now here I am still awake at three o clock in the morning. Sleep at this point wasn't an option. Gabby's face kept invading my dreams. I sat up and swung my legs over the side of the bed and stretched. Fatigue was starting to set in and I felt a little dizzy. I took a sip of the warm water that set on my stand before attempting to stand up. I gathered myself before heading downstairs.

I found myself in the kitchen staring at the contents in my freezer. I grabbed the carton of Breyer's ice cream and held it in my hand. I stood there with the freezer door open, too scared to close it because I knew she was there. It was dark but just enough moonlight flashed through the kitchen window. I swallowed the lump in my throat and just stood there, as cold air blanketed my face.

My heart rate quickened and the fear gripping my heart almost caused my bladder to fold. Maybe this shit is all in my head but I didn't even touch the freezer door it just closed on its own. And just like I suspected she was there. I didn't even realize I dropped the container of ice cream until I heard the carton hit the floor with a thud. My body started shaking; I was too scared to look at her.

She hasn't bothered me in years. This was all Detective Harley's fault. He summoned her spirit, now here she is bothering me. Finally I turned and looked at her. I knew she wasn't going anywhere until I finally acknowledged her ass. She looked just like I left her, soak and wet. She still had on her pink pajamas, her hair pulled back into a pony tail. She looked just like Savannah only a couple of shades lighter. She put up one hell of a fight to, but my determination to get rid of her defeated her battle to live.

It took a long time for me to get rid of her spirit the first go around. She was my first kill and for a while it weighed on my conscious, but eventually I learned to cope with what I did and she eventually went away. I wondered why the hell she decided to pop up now.

I was always jealous of Gabby. I wanted Savannah all to myself and it seemed I couldn't have that with Gabby around. She was always in the way. She always wanted to tag along with me and Savannah wherever we went. That shit got annoying after a while. To the point where I had no choice but to kill her . . . so I did. It was me who convinced her to get out of bed and take a walk down to the pond. She trusted me and had no worries. I think Mom Karen had a lingering suspicion about me being involved because she treated me differently after Gabby died.

"Roxie," she called my name in that annoying ass voice of hers.

"What?" I snapped. "What do you want now Gabby?" I whined.

"Just to let you know it will all be over soon," she smiled, and then laughed this creepy drawn out laugh. The fucked up part, I started laughing right along with her ass.

Brian

My alarm clock sounded and I knew it was time for me to get my day started. My body was still tired, since I didn't get much sleep the night before. I leaned over and took my frustrations out on my alarm clock. I didn't realize I hit it that hard until I heard it crash to the floor. I sat up and looked at it briefly before laying back down to stare up at the ceiling. Loneliness crept up on me as I caressed the empty spot beside me, Savannah's spot. I can count on my hands how many times she has graced my bed with her presence. I waited five months to get the goods and seems like I'm still fighting for it. A man of my stature should never have to beg for pussy.

It's a damn shame how much I love that girl. It's a over-bearing, strong, suffocating, damn near a deadly kind of love, but I can't help how I love. When I love I love hard but she doesn't appreciate all the love I'm willing to give. Women always crying that sad story about how they want a *good* black man, but when they get one they don't know how to treat him.

My emotions were starting to take over and that's not a good thing. I shook off the deadly and negative thoughts that surrounded my head. For now I would keep my distance. I love Savannah and I don't want to hurt her, but I knew that's what my current state of mind was leading me to do. I have a psychological condition, and I hear these voices in my head sometimes. When I take my medication they leave me alone for the most part, but lately I've been slipping. I just hate the way the medication makes me feel, or maybe I just need an excuse to act on my deadly impulses.

Tired of feeling like a bitch in their feelings I got up, took a shower and headed to the office. I own a popular dance club, my father passed on to me a few years ago. I run it along with my brother Ace. I pulled up to the building and of course no one is here since it's a Wednesday. Our hours of operation are generally

Thursday through Sunday. I walked through the quiet building and headed straight to my office.

As soon as I sat down I opened up my desk and pulled out my buddy Jack Daniels. I took the cap off and took a huge gulp. It stung a little as it washed down my throat but I needed it. I sat there staring at my computer for hours unable to get a damn thing done. I grabbed my phone off my desk and searched through my call log and text messages to see if anything came through from Savannah . . . nothing. I took a deep breath to suppress my anger. I took the bottle of Jack Daniels off my desk and took another huge gulp.

"Damn I hope she don't make me kill her ass," I said out loud.

"Agreed," I said answering myself as I nodded my head in agreement.

*****

"Yo' Brian, did you hear what I said?" Ace asked me as he leaned back in the chair opposite me folding his arms across his chest. I could tell by the serious frown on his face that he was getting frustrated, and he's only been here ten minutes.

"My bad," I said shaking my head and rubbing my hand over a fresh set of waves. Ace looked at me and shook his head. "Just repeat the question," I said to my older brother of three months. We have the same father different mothers. People say we look a lot alike and we are often mistaken for twins.

"I said did you beef up the security?" he snapped running his tongue over his teeth.

I sighed and closed my eyes because I didn't. We're making preparations for a party we are throwing at the club this Friday with the music artist Wale as the special guest. We always beef up on security whenever we have a celebrity guest. Groupies and I guess THOTS is the new word for them now days, be extra so we make sure we have extra security just to be on the safe side.

"B, what is up with you man?" Ace asked me shaking his head. I could see the disappointment in his face as he looked at me. "I'm going to need you to get it together. It's like you not even here? You got me repeating myself and shit. You know I hate when I have to ask a question twice."

"I said my bad."

"I'm just saying, you know that I've handled everything else. I got the dancers, the alcohol, the flyers, and tickets. The only thing you had to do is make sure we have extra security and make sure the sound is straight and you can't even handle that. I might as well run this shit by my damn self." He was testing my patience and he knew it.

"I get it Ace, damn," I snapped biting the inside of my jaw.

"It's Savannah," he said shaking his head. He chuckled a little before stroking his jaw like he was in deep thought.

"What?" I questioned.

"She's bad news Brian."

"That's my wife."

"In what fairytale nigga," he barked. I knew he was mad. I could tell by the veins that popped out of his neck. He had a temper like me and at times we butted heads but we're brothers; we never stay mad at each other for long. I let his remark slide.

"Can we get back to business or do you want to continue to discuss my love life?"

e shook his head before looking at me. "This shit not healthy for you B. You got a good thing going; no we got a good thing going and you about to fuck it up."

"Ace-,"

"Did you do it?" he asked cutting me off.

"Huh?" I frowned.

"Did you do it?" he repeated. "Did you kill that girl parent's Brian?" I placed my head in my hands. I couldn't bring myself to look at him as I answered.

"Yes." I heard him sigh, but I really didn't have a choice. It was the only way to keep Savannah from leaving me. Earlier that day me and Savannah were having a serious conversation. I felt we'd been together long enough to take our relationship to the next level. She kept feeding me that bullshit about wanting to take things slow, but I've been more than patient and I was getting tired of waiting. I suggested we move in together, that's when out of the blue she says "We need to talk". It was the way she said it, and I knew shit between us was about to get real. So I did what I had to do. Don't judge me I'm not the only nigga out here who has done some crazy shit for love.

I looked up at Ace. I could see the disappointment in his eyes as he shook his head. Once again I had left him hanging because of Savannah. I was supposed to be handling business with him that day. We dibble and dabble in the drug game so that day in particular we were supposed to be setting an example when one of our runners when his money came up short but Savannah tried to drop the bomb on me so I had to do something. I could try to explain my actions but it would be useless. Ace would never understand. He has never been in love like I've been in love.

"That shit was reckless Brian," he barked at me.

"I covered my tracks. Besides they don't think I had anything to do with it. I don't have a cloud of suspicion hanging over my head," I smirked as I thought about Roxie. I can't stand her stuck up ass. Savannah can't see it but that bitch is just as crazy in love with her like I am. It's only a matter of time before the process of elimination will begin and it's going to be either me or her. I'm gonna do everything possible to make sure it's not me. I just have to bide my time for now.

"I don't understand you B?"

"I know you don't."

"All this pussy out here and you tripping' off one."

"It's more than sex Ace. I love that girl," I said, but I could tell by the frown on his face that he wasn't trying to hear it."

"Just like you loved Macy, huh?"

I sat back and allowed the tension between us to grow a little thicker. Macy, an ex girlfriend of mine reminded me a lot of Savannah. She was beautiful, smart and independent. I fell hard for her also, but somewhere in our relationship things kind of went left. I think it had something to do with the fact I may have had a hand in the fact her brother Joe Rock's club was unsuccessful.

Since I'm telling the story I might as well come clean. I did have something to do with Club Essence as he called it coming to an end. His club was becoming a hot commodity, it was making some noise and I'm not gone lie I felt threatened. I made some phone calls, I had the fire Marshall's come out there and illegally shut his club down a few times. I guess people got tired of wasting their money. He couldn't really compete after that. Don't shake your head at me. It's a cold world out here, you either sink or swim. I'm not drowning for nobody.

So Macy tried to leave me, but I couldn't let that happen. I loved her too much. If I couldn't have her I made sure nobody else could either. So I killed her. Her brother was a bonus. He was just in the wrong place at the wrong time.

"You putting everything we built in jeopardy," Ace snapped rocking me out of my thoughts. "You about to lose all of this over some-,"

I jumped out of my seat before he could finish his sentence. I leaned forward and placed my forearms on my desk as I looked at him. For the first time a hint of fear danced across his eyes. Ace has never been scared of me, but today I saw something different in his eyes.

"Don't disrespect her," I said in serious tone. He breathed in deep and ran his tongue across his teeth.

"All I'm saying is don't get caught up in another case."

"In what case? Have they found any bodies?" I asked with a cold smirk. They won't either. I chopped up their bodies and fed them to the fish.

"That don't mean shit B and you know it. You don't think they won't come checking for you if another girlfriend of yours comes up missing? You got to think Brian," he said jabbing at his head with his index finger.

"It won't come to that." He shook his head at me like he knew something that I didn't.

"She doesn't love you B. I just want what's best for you. . . Just let her go." A brief pause settled between us before he continued. "She's gone be your down fall B." He said it with so much conviction it made my heart jump, but I quickly shook it off.

"I appreciate you looking out for me but believe me when I say I got this." He sighed and shook his head.

"Aight man, lets get back to business," he said finally deciding to drop the subject.

"I like the sound of that," I said nodding my head and rubbing my hands together.

"You don't plan on bringing Savannah to Miami with us?" he asked.

Miami! I thought to myself. I don't know what the hell he's talking about so to save his face I play it off.

"I've thought about it. I think it would do us both some good. She's been through a lot, with losing her parent's." He looked at me sideways.

"Look what's done is done, ain't no need in feeling guilty," he muttered.

"Who says I do?" He shook his head.

"You cold B."

"So is life," I shrugged.

"Look, I just think it will be better for both of us if you leave Savannah at home, but it's on you. We leave Sunday."

The more he talked my memory came back to me as to why we were heading to Miami. In the past Ace and I have talked about expanding. We wanted to start a few more clubs, but I thought we discussed the first club would be in New York.

"I've seen a few pictures of the location, it's located right off the beach. I think this is a good investment B. Shit I might move down there just to get away from yo' crazy ass. I ain't trying to get caught up in *your* bull shit." We laughed but I knew he was dead serious.

"You ain't no saint."

"Compared to you I am." We shared another laugh. "If everything goes as planned opening night will be New Year's Eve."

"That soon huh?" I asked rubbing my chin.

"It gives us roughly two months and some change to pull this shit off. If you stay focused and get Big Brian to pull some strings we can get shit straight as far as the liquor license, the permit, etcetera, etcetera."

I frowned at the thought of having to ask my father for anything. I hated him with a passion. Yeah he handed the club over to me but it was well deserved. All the years of hustling for his ass, this was owed to me. All the late nights early mornings, running packages, working in trap houses for free. I could have went down hard if I ever got caught. That alone shows how much my father cared about me. He was a heavy hitter in the game and used the club as a front. Kind of like me but I wanted to expand, so I can put this drug shit behind me. I want a family one day and I would never subject my children to the things my father subjected me to.

"I'm thinking we can get somebody like Tahiry, or Erica Mena, or even Cyn from Love and Hip Hop to headline the party. I'm leaning towards Cyn, she's a bad bitch."

"You got this all figured out I see."

"Yeah nigga I'm ready to do this. You know me, my mind stay ticking like clock work. I already talked to Damon. He's meeting us down there," he said referring to my lawyer. "Matter of fact you should let Prince come with us. He might learn a thing or two."

I smirked. Prince is my litter brother. We have the same mother different fathers. Ace had a point about bringing Prince with us. His spoiled ass always talking about opening up a club one day, he wanted to part ownership of mines. I laughed at that shit. He doesn't know anything about hard work. While both of our fathers our successful business men, I worked hard for everything I got while Prince had everything handed to him. I glanced down at my new Rolex watch and checked the time.

"Matter of fact he should have been here by now. I told him to come by I have a few errands I wanted him to run."

"I'm not surprised. You know how he is. He probably snuggled up with Roxie's gold digging ass."

"Yep, but it won't be for long."

*****

Savannah hates when I stop by her house unannounced but it don't stop me from doing it. I parked my Lexus right behind her truck and hopped out of the car. I zipped up my jacket to keep out the slight chill of the October weather. The time on my Rolex read it was almost nine o clock. She's probably tired after working her usual twelve hour shift, but knowing her she's probably up reading a book. She hasn't been sleeping all that good since her parents died.

I walked up to the door debating on whether or not I should use the key I made. I decided against it since Savannah had no clue that I even have a key to her house. In the midst of everything, with Savannah being so distraught over her parents I was able to sneak off with her house key and have one made for myself. I am her man, so I should have a key to her place especially since she has a key to mine. I knocked on the door, and waited at least a good five minutes with no response so I knocked again.

After a few more minutes went by with no response I really got in my feelings and pounded on the door. A light flicked on. I could hear her foot steps as she approached.

"Who is it?" she snapped. I had a feeling she already knew it was me but I answered her ass anyway.

"Brian." She opened the door partially and looked me up and down like I'm some random nigga off the street.

"What do you want Brian? Why didn't you call first?" she asked. She looked like she'd been crying. My heart immediately softened. I hate the fact that I was probably the cause of her tears but I didn't have a choice. She forced my hand so I played it.

"What's wrong baby?" I asked forcing my way in without properly being invited.

I wrapped my arms around her waist. She laid her head on my chest and damn near crumbled in my arms. I picked her up. Why the hell I did that I don't even know. I mean I'm a nice sized dude standing at six one but Savannah is five nine. She's not a big girl but she ain't little either. It was a struggle carrying her up the steps but with the good Lord's help we made it.

I gently laid her down on the bed then laid down beside her. She placed her head on my chest. I didn't even have to ask I already knew what the tears were about. Silence devoured us as she silently cried herself to sleep. I stroked her hair and kissed her forehead. Seeing Savannah like this fucked with my heart. Like the saying goes time heals all wounds, I know eventually this to shall pass.

For some reason I'm restless and can't sleep. I looked down at Savannah and watched her as she slept. Damn, she's beautiful. I know I have to be the luckiest man in the world to have someone like her on arm. I plan to do everything within my means to keep it that way. Careful not to wake her I slid out of bed and headed to her bathroom. I relieved my bladder, washed my face and hands. Savannah was still sleep so I figured I would cook her some breakfast to cheer her up a little. She still had her work clothes on so she must have been having a rough day yesterday. Her usual routine after working is to grab a bite to eat then head straight to the shower.

I was just wrapping up the breakfast that I made for her when I heard her enter the kitchen. I shook my head because only Savannah would have a nigga doing shit like this. I don't think I ever cooked for Macy.

"Hungry?" I asked her, as I placed the dirty dishes in the dishwater.

"Not really," she said sitting down at the table.

"Well, just try to eat something," I suggested as I grabbed the plate I fixed for her out of the warmer. I watched as her eyes betrayed whatever thoughts she had before. I fixed sausage, pancakes, bacon, eggs, and grits.

"Okay," she smiled up at me. I bent down and kissed her forehead. Her eyes were a little swollen but that did little to take away from her beauty.

"You want to talk about it?" I asked taking a seat beside her. She shook her head no. "It might do some good to talk about it instead of keeping everything bottled up."

"Brian," she sighed. I held my hands up in defense mode. "Okay, I won't press the issue."

"Thank you."

"You know what would cheer you up?" She looked at me sideways and rolled her eyes. I guess that came out wrong. I understand she would rather have her parent's back but this might be a good substitute for now. "Ace and I are flying down to Miami Sunday. It would be my pleasure if you would join me."

"Huh? You never mentioned anything about Miami." That's not the reaction I was looking for but I still ran with it.

"Yeah, Ace and I are trying to expand. We plan on opening a club down there." Her nonchalant demeanor was throwing me off. Maybe I was expecting too much.

"I can't Brian."

"Why not?"

"Because I do have a job. I can't just take off and go on some vacation. It doesn't work like that."

"I keep telling you, you don't need that job Savannah."

"I like my job Brian."

"So pretty much fuck it, right. You not going?" She shook her head. I pinched the bridge of my nose.

Shit like this bruised my ego. Why couldn't she be like every other chick I've dated? If it were any other bitch, me telling them to quit their job would be like music to their ears. Don't get me wrong I found Savannah's independence attractive at one point and time, but now it's starting to piss me off.

"Can you give it some thought?"

"No," she said shaking her head. "I'm just not in the mood for a vacation. I just buried my parents Brian."

"And taking a vacation right now makes perfect sense."

"Fine I'll think about it," she said, but I wasn't convinced. I think she only said it to shut me up.

Maybe it's time for me make her start missing me. I bet if I ignore her ass while I'm down in Miami that will wake her up and quick. I'm tired of being the one to always call, and try to make time for *us*. Let's see how Savannah likes a little reverse psychology. I heard laughter in my head.

"That ain't gone work."

"Shut the fuck up," I mumbled under my breath.

Roxie

"Strike!" Zaheeda yelled pumping her fist in the air. I rolled my eyes at the silliness. She must have caught me because she cocked her head sideways and smirked. "Don't hate," she said curling up her top lip placing her hand on her hip. I was just about to address her ass but Vee decided to intervene.

"Chick please, ain't nobody hatin' on you,"
We were all chilling at the bowling alley for a girl's outing. It was actually Zaheeda the bull idea. I still can't stand Zaheeda and I know the feeling is mutual. We try to remain cordial because of Vee. It's a struggle especially when she comes at me sideways with her slick ass comments. We are grown women; I wish she'd act like it.

"Please, I can see it in ya eyes boo."

"Chick get over yourself," Vee laughed as she stood and inspected which ball she wanted.

Watching Vee was comical. She tested about three balls before settling on an orange one. She breathed deep and held the ball up to her chin. You should have seen her ass. I swear she thinks she is a damn professional. With slow and calculated steps she walked towards the lane. She took five steps and let the ball fly. All that and guess what she still rolled a gutter ball. Zaheeda and I fell out laughing.

"I thought you said bowling was one of your hobbies?" Zaheeda laughed.

"It is. I'm just a little rusty," Vee said cocking her head to the side.

"Whatever."

"Roxie, it's your turn," Vee said turning to me.

"Let me show you how's it's done Vee," I said standing up. I grabbed the same ball as Vee, did the exact routine she did and guess what . . . ya girl got a strike. I fist pumped the air and did little twerk move. "Strike."

"Roxie," Vee said looking around. "Its children in here," she whispered under her breath. I jerked my neck back like I'd been punched in the throat.

"So, what they got to do with me? They ain't mine."

"She does have a point, and thank God for that," Zaheeda added.

I swear she almost made me go there with her ass. She was getting real reckless with her mouth. All I do is try to stay in my lane and mind my own business. It's bitches like her that cause bitches like me to act hostile. I stood in front of her with my hand on my hip. Visions of me wrapping my hand around her throat and punishing her face with my fist vividly flashed before my eyes.

"Aye, you aight?" Zaheeda asked me.

"Yeah, I'm good but I'd be even better if you keep your little comments to yourself. I'm too old to play with other peoples kids."

"Touché," she said running her tongue across her teeth. "Its all in fun boo. No shade."

"Yeah, I bet," I said plopping down in the chair beside Vee.

"Really?" Vee asked looking at Zaheeda before looking at me. "Can we come out, have a day of fun without all the bullshit? Damn," Vee asked shaking her head.

It got quiet between us real quick. That was so unlike Vee to come off like that. We must have really pissed her off.

"I'm sorry Vee," I said rubbing her knee.

"Me too," Zaheeda added. "You're right. Roxie we may not like each other and that's cool, but we can be cordial. I promise I won't throw anymore shade, or tea, or lemonade." That got a laugh out of Vee. Gosh I love that girl smile.

"Same here Zaheeda."

"Good, cause I came out to have a good time. That's all that's on my mind," Vee sang as she snapped her fingers.

"Naw boo stick to your day job," Zaheeda laughed.

"Agreed," I chimed in.

"Oh, tell Brian thank you for hooking us up in VIP last night. Girl Wale was all over me wasn't he?" Zaheeda asked

"Hell no," Vee laughed.

"I know but at least he took a picture with me," she laughed. I kept my comments to myself because I sure did leave his hotel room this morning. That's the only thing Brian is good for though. He knows a few people in the music industry.

"Guys," Savannah sighed.

"Yeah," both Zaheeda and I answered in unison.

"I've been thinking a lot lately, and . . . I think I want to move. I think it's time for me to leave the Eastern Shore."

I swear it felt like the air had been sucked out of my lungs. Did Vee just say she wanted to move? I would be all for it if she said I could go with her but I have a feeling that me tagging along is nowhere in the plans. Vee you can't leave me, I would go crazy. I was the first to speak.

"Why?" I asked in a strained voice. I was on the verge of tears and I could see Zaheeda looking at me but her thoughts and feelings regarding me were irrelevant.

"Because, I just feel like there is nothing left for me here," she confessed. To hear her say that hurt like hell. It was like I didn't mean shit to her.

"I think it's a great idea," Zaheeda said nodding her head. I jerked my neck and looked at her. She shrugged her shoulders. "It might do you some good to get away, just as long as you're not running away." Vee frowned.

"What would I be running away from?" Vee asked.

"I don't know, it just sounded good at the moment." Vee shook her head and laughed. "Any idea on where you want to go?"

"Georgia?"

"Why Georgia?"

"I've always wanted to move down there. The cost of living is cheaper and I heard it's a nice place to live."

"What about Brian?" Zaheeda smirked.

"What about him?" Vee asked smacking her lips.

"You know good and damn well you ain't leaving that man."

"Anyway," Vee said as she sucked her teeth and rolled her eyes.

They were too wrapped up in their conversation to even notice me. At that moment I felt like the wind had been knocked out of me. I couldn't breathe, my heart was racing, and everything seemed to spinning in circles. How could Vee play me like this?

How could she so easily walk out on over ten years of friendship? My lack of self control couldn't stop the tears from falling from my eyes. Vee finally got over herself and decided to give me some attention.

"Roxie what's wrong?" she asked me. She had the nerve to act like she really cared. I knew I had to get it together. I took a few deep breaths and wiped the tears from my eyes.

"So you just gone up and leave?" She screwed up her face. Why should I care about her feelings when she doesn't care about mines? "What about me . . . what about us?"

After I said my peace it seemed everything got quiet. Vee gave me this weird look like I'm crazy or something, but I'm use to it. I have every right to feel this way. Now she's sitting here on mute, when just a few minutes ago she was chatty patty. My question deserved an answer.

"Awkward," Zaheeda sang as she stood up. "I'm going to the bathroom. I think you two need some *alone* time," she giggled. I don't find a damn thing funny. I rolled my eyes as I watched her fake Indian wanna be ass walk away.

Vee still hadn't bothered to address the situation and I needed answers. She's all I got. Where she's goes, I go whether she approves or not. After a few odd minutes of silence she decided to break the ice.

"I just need a fresh start Roxie."

"We can start over together," I quickly shot back.

I sounded desperate, maybe I am. I could tell by her facial expression that it was rubbing her the wrong way. It didn't matter because her thoughts on the matter were dead to me. Vee fails to realize that she will never be able to get away from me. I can't live without her, and I was going to do everything in my power to make sure she can't live without me.

"It's not even that serious Roxie. Nothing is set in stone. It was just a thought," she said rolling her eyes.

"What's with the attitude?"

"Nothing," she snapped, as she bent over and took off her bowling shoes.

"So you mad now?"

"Nope, I'm good," she said standing up.

Her attitude about the whole situation isn't sitting well with me. See that's the shit I don't like. Now she all up in her feelings for nothing. If anybody should be mad it's me. I could feel myself ready to take it there with Vee, so I said a silent prayer that the Lord will keep me in my right frame of mind.

"So ya'll straight?" Zaheeda asked deciding to bring her unwanted ass back to join us. She looked from Vee to me.

"Yep," Vee said standing up and leaving me there with lingering questions. My first thought was to go after her but I decided to give her, her space for now.

"Just curious Roxie are you looking for more than just a friendship with Savannah?"

"What?" I looked up at this bitch and my top lip immediately curled. She wanted me to go with there with her. I knew I had to put some distance between me and this chick, and quick.

"You heard me."

"You've known me all of two minutes, don't ask me no dumb ass shit like that." I can't stand fake bitches. Just a minute ago she was talking that mess about being cordial and no more throwing shade. Bitches change like they change niggas.

"Hey, I'm just trying to help you out. I don't want your little feelings to get hurt. We all know how dramatic Roxie gets."

This bitch was really trying me. But the way she said that last sentence touched a nerve. It made me question if Vee use to sit up and talk about me with this bitch. The more I looked at her the more my hands started to twitch. If I didn't remove myself from the situation I have a feeling I would end up in jail tonight.

"Bye," I said standing up. I was over this conversation. Do you know this linebacker had the nerve to block my path? She had about two inches on me but it didn't stop me from looking her up and down. "Move.!"

"Roxie. . . Roxie," she sighed. You may have Savannah fooled but not me. I know you killed her parents. I don't know how but I'm going to prove it."

She had me fucked up. See this is why I only rocks with Vee because of chickens like this. I try to keep my crazy under wraps but a random bitch always finds a way to pull it out of me. It's obvious this bitch sent for me, she ain't going to like how I answer that ass.

"Sweetheart, whether I did or not is no concern of yours. Messing in other peoples business is bad for your health. See that's what's wrong with the world today, bitches don't know how to stay in their own lane keep swerving in shit that doesn't concern you, that's how people get killed."

"Are you threatening me?"

"I don't do threats boo. That's just a waste of time and energy. Now this is your final warning please move, or be moved." I didn't even give her a chance to respond. I couldn't resist as I kindly shoved her out of my way. I guess I shoved her ass hard too because she went flying backwards. I kept it moving and didn't even bother to look back. I know her type, all bark no bite. I should've head butted her ass.

*****

It's another sleepless night for me. Once again Gabby has decided to grace me with her presence. She's irritating the hell out of me. I can't even take a piss, or properly wipe my ass without her standing there watching me like a damn hawk. A place that should give me peace and serenity has become my private hell within a matter of days. I flipped through the channels on my television trying to ignore her and keep what little bit of sanity I had left. I was hoping for some company tonight but Bri's working, and once again Prince is busy. He's starting to piss me off. I plan on making it my business to find out who or what is keeping him so busy. I didn't want him to begin with but I'm not use to niggas dissing me. It's usually the other way around. Just for a moment I had peace because my thoughts allowed me to drift from the unnatural spirit corrupting my state of mind but a cool breeze that danced across my face brought me back to the present. Another cold chill rolled off my spine.

I turned to her and gave her the screw face, but she continued to give me that creepy ass smile. I wonder why she resurfaced after all these years. I know I'm crazy but as I looked at her and I wondered just how crazy.

"Why are you here Gabby?" I finally asked. I'm tired cranky and just want some sleep.

"It's almost over," she replied.

"You keep saying that. Why the fuck do you keep saying that?" I yelled, but she just continued to smile. Anger consumed me and I started to shake. I need help. If I don't get rid of Gabby and soon I know I'm going to lose it. "Gabby please, just leave me alone," I begged. I could feel the tears as they rolled off my cheeks.

"You can make this all go away, Roxie," she said and smiled. I sat up and looked at her.

"Please, tell me. I'll do anything." This shit is pathetic. Here I am begging a dead girl's ghost to leave me alone. If this shit ain't crazy I don't know what the hell is.

"Just tell the truth, and your conscious will be clear." I looked at her sideways. That's not even an option. She's crazy for even suggesting some shit like that.

"Huh?"

"It's time for you to come clean about everything Roxie. About me, about Brandon . . . and the baby." I screwed up my face in confusion.

"What baby?"

Savannah's baby."

Savannah

I swear the people in my life are certified. I can't believe Roxie and Zaheeda acted like pure dee fools. The last time I checked we are adults, its time they both started acting like it. I expect a lot of dramatics from Roxie, but Zaheeda participating in the bull threw me for a loop. I can only shake my head at the foolery. I have enough drama in my life I don't need anymore.

A knock came at the door rocking me out of my thoughts. I already knew who it was. I couldn't help as my eyes rolled into the back of my head. Brian is leaving for Miami tomorrow so he wants us to spend some alone time together before he leaves. The smart thing to do is end this thing now. Zaheeda is right about one thing, I need to stop being so nice to people. I'm always putting other people and their feelings before my own. As much as I hated to do this I had too. It's not fair to him. I sighed as I stood up and headed towards the door. I opened the door and my heart dropped. Brian stood there with a big bouquet of red and white roses.

"A rose for a rose," he said peeking around the bouquet he held in his hand.

"Thanks," I said trying hard to sound appreciative. Here I go feeling like shit. I just lost my nerve. How can I break up with a guy who just brought me roses?

"What's wrong baby?" he asked walking in and kissing me on the forehead. I took the flowers out of his hand and shook my head.

"Nothing, baby just a little tired." I placed the flowers in the kitchen before joining him in the living room. I sat down beside him.

As always he smelled and looked good. He's rocking a fresh cut; he had on a black Armani sweater, paired up with black Armani jeans. A silver chain hung around his neck enhancing his smooth chocolate complexion. Damn this man is fine, but I think that's where the attraction ended. It was just physical nothing deeper, well at least from my side of things.

The evening actually didn't go to bad. We chilled, ordered take out because your girl don't do much cooking and sipped on some wine. He still tried to persuade me to go to Miami with him and as tempting as it sounds I'm just not in the mood to go. A vacation would probably do me some good but my heart isn't in it.

We've been hugged up on the couch for a good three hours. It's a little past eleven o' clock. Everything was good until I felt him squeeze my ass. I'm so glad he couldn't see my face because my eyes sure did disappear into the back of my head. He then moved my hair and started planting soft kisses on the back of neck. I knew what that meant.

Our sex life has been put on hold since my parents passed away. Too much was going on to even think about it and it wasn't fair to Brian. But the fact this nigga can't fuck isn't fair to me either. He groped my breast, and massaged my nipples as he continued to kiss on my neck. I know he's looking for some type of reaction, but I can't bring myself to give him one. My sensitive parts betrayed me though. His touch caused moisture to form between my legs. I could feel my pearl pulsate. A nice nut would definitely be what the doctor prescribed but Brian's whack ass sex just doesn't have what it takes to fill the prescription. I continued to look at television laughing out loud at Martin to show him I was the least bit interested hoping he would get the hint, he didn't.

The next thing I know we are upstairs in my bedroom. I say a good ten minutes later I'd just experienced yet another episode of bad sex one o one. I slid out of bed while he laid up here sleep next to me like what we just did was special. I needed to take a shower. I'm too old to be putting myself through this shit.

It was a little after one in the morning when Brian woke me up out of my sleep and told me he was about to leave. He had to go pick up Ace and head to the airport. Of course he tried to convince me to go with him but again I declined.

"Baby," he said caressing the side of my face.

"Yeah," I yawned.

"Will you give us moving in together some thought?"

"Brian, I'm not ready. I like having my own space. I like the way things are right now. We already had this discussion and you keep pressing the issue." I sighed. Once again I'm so over this conversation. Maybe starting up this club in Miami is what he need. He said he will be down there for at least two weeks and will probably be back and forth for the next couple of months until the grand opening New Years Eve. It's sad to say but that was like music to my ears.

"Okay Savannah," he responded. I could tell he was disappointed. His disposition softened. I had a feeling he was about to say the three forbidden words again but I can't let that happen. I grabbed the back of his head and kissed him.

"Be safe babe. Call me when you get there." I quickly said and rolled over on my side giving him my back. He kissed the top of my head.

"I love you Savannah."

I knew he was still there waiting for me to respond and that's when I made my decision. Tears glossed over my eyes because I couldn't do this to him nor myself anymore. I rolled over and sat up. This is going to be hard. He's had my back and has been very supportive since my parent's died, but I can't continue on with this relationship. He noticed the tears in my eyes.

"What's wrong Savannah?" he asked wiping the tears that fell from my eyes.

"We need to talk," I sighed wiping my tears away.

"Is everything okay."

"Brian, I can't do this anymore," I finally said after a brief pause. He just continued to look at me with this a strange expression on his face. "Brian, did you hear what I just said?"

"What do you mean you can't do *this* anymore?"

"Brian you're a nice guy and I know you will make some woman happy one day, but that woman won't be me."

"Savannah please don't say that," he said grabbing my hand. "I love you."

"That's just it Brian, I don't love you."

"You will grow to love me," he pleaded. This is harder than I thought. "Don't give up on us yet. Maybe this trip to Miami might do us some good. We just need a little break."

"Brian," I sighed.

"Please, Savannah."

"I don't think-,"

"Just think about it," he barked at me and I jumped. He had this look in his eyes it was a mixture of pain, and anger. For some reason my mother's words popped in my head. *He ain't right Savannah* she said to me not to long before she died. I swallowed the lump in my throat. I slid my hand underneath my pillow and made sure my handy knife is still in place. She is. I hate confrontation so I avoid it as much as possible but if I have to I can hand out some whoop ass. I should've stopped him at the damn door and told him it was over, but nope I didn't want to hurt his feelings. Now here it is damn near two o clock in the morning and I'm putting up with a man who is clearly in his feelings.

Dumb Savannah.

"Okay," I whispered just to pacify him and get him out of my house. He could leave for a month and my decision would still remain the same. He smiled.

"We can talk when I get back." I nodded my head yes and he bent down and kissed me on the forehead. "I love you Savannah."

I remained unmoved as he walked out of the door. As soon as I heard the door close I let out the breath I was holding. I stayed put for a few seconds before grabbing the knife underneath my pillow. I made sure the front door was locked and set my alarm something I rarely do. I walked back into my bedroom and locked that door too. I felt some what relieved although I know this isn't the last of Brain. Hopefully while he is down in Miami it will finally register that it's over but who knows. Honestly I don't feel as bad as I thought I would.

I lay down on my bed and welcome the darkness that suddenly seemed to surround me. I wrapped my blanket tighter around my body, but that did little to comfort me. Thoughts of my parents and little sister entered my head without permission. I hate when I have moments like this. I could feel the tears coming on and as hard as I tried I couldn't stop them.

I curled tighter into the fetal position and let out a gut wrenching cry. The kind of cry that makes your body shake. I missed them like crazy. I would give anything to just hear my mother's laughter, to see Gabby smile, and to jump into my daddies arms again. I cried until I couldn't cry no more. The pain was unbearable, to the point it was driving me insane. There was only one thing left for me to do. I rolled off my bed and dropped to my knees, and began to pray.

*****

After church service I felt a little bit better. The Pastor preached about trial and tribulations and that God gives the hardest battles to his toughest warriors. I want to think of myself as tough but here lately my emotions have been getting the best of me. I want to stand strong because that's what my parent's would want me to do, but it gets hard at times.

Thank heavens traffic was light and I made it to work in no time. The charge nurse text me and asked me if I could come in because one of the nurses on duty had to leave due to a family emergency. I was all for it. Any distraction to keep my mind off of the sadness and drama that surrounded my life right now would do. Imagine my surprise when I bumped into Zaheeda.

"Hey Savannah," she spoke to me as I sat down at my station.

"Hey," I said shortly logging onto my computer.

"Don't be like that Savannah."

"Like what?" I asked, shrugging my shoulders like I didn't know what she was talking about. She sighed.

"I'm sorry about what happened between me and Roxie the other day. It was childish and uncalled for."

"Right it was. I expect shit like that from Roxie but you Zee. I love Roxie to pieces but sometimes she can be a little over the top and you're like a breath of fresh air. I thought you were someone I could talk to without all the drama. Guess I was wrong," I said shrugging my shoulders.

"Okay, wait. You sound like one of those soap opera chicks. You watch way too much tv."

"I'm serious Zee," I said giving her the side eye trying to suppress a laugh.

"I'm just saying, but you're right. Shit between Roxie and I got way out of hand. I shouldn't have came at her like that, but something ain't right about her Savannah. I know that's ya girl and all but I just want you to be careful. You're like a sister to me and I would hate to see anything bad happen to you," she leaned over and gave me a hug.

"Just let me worry about Roxie."

"Aight, just be careful," she said standing up.

"Where you going?"

"My shift is over boo. Donna called me to come in this morning. I think a bug or something is going around, two nurses called out this morning."

"Ugh!" I said grabbing my sanitizer and dousing my hands in it. "It would be my luck to get sick."

"I know right. So other than the usual shit how are you feeling? You look tired, are you getting enough sleep?"

"I'm good and sleep comes and goes at times. I still have a lot on my mind. My parent's killer is still out there roaming free. Sometimes I feel like I might be next."

"Don't talk like that," Zee frowned.

"I know," I sighed. "So how's it looking for me tonight?" I asked changing the subject to remove the dark cloud that hovered over my head.

"Not too much. We sent one lady back home," Zee laughed. "She was pissed too, she cussed Stacy out," Zee said shaking her head. "I tried not to laugh but it was too funny. You should have seen the look on Stacy's face. I think she only held her cool because Donna was in house, but if Laura was here she would have gave it right back to her." I nodded my head in agreement. Both Donna and Laura are Charge nurses however Donna took a lot more shit than Laura did.

"I hope whoever she is stay her grouchy ass home. Humph I might just give it right back to her ass tonight." Zaheeda looked at me sideways and laughed.

"Girl bye. Aight chicka I'm ready to blow this joint. You like night shift?" she frowned.

"It doesn't bother me."

"Well, it bother's me. It takes away from my beauty sleep. It takes a lot to look like this," she said waving her hand over her face. I shook my head and laughed.

"Girl, bye."

"Don't hate," she said grabbing her bag and throwing it over her shoulder. "Call me later."

"Okay."

By eleven thirty that evening I helped deliver two babies and I was drained. I love my job but those two women were like two peas in a pod, or maybe I'm insensitive because I have no idea what it's like to be in actual labor. If you count my miscarriage but I don't think that's even close enough to compare, but oh my gosh the two I had to deal with were whiny. Candi was the worst though. Do you know this chick was one push away from delivering her baby and she gave up? She literally laid there and refused to push anymore, so of course Dr. Wadi the doctor on call had to perform a C –section. I could tell by his facial expression that he was heated, but karmas a bitch because his attitude is just as ugly as he is.

My buzzer rang taking me away from my chart work. I looked up and noticed it was Gabby short for Gabrielle. She came in an hour ago, her water broke and she's already four to five centimeters dilated. It just wasn't the name but for some reason she reminded me of my sister Gabby. I don't know if it's her beautiful bright doe eyes or just her sunny disposition.

"Yes," I said into the intercom.

"Can you check me again please?"

"Sure I'm on my way."

When I entered Gabby's room her husband was right by her side, wiping stray beads of sweat off her face. They're both young, he's twenty-three and she just turned twenty-one but it's obvious they are happy in love. I couldn't help but to smile at them as my thoughts drifted to Brandon. This could have been us, no this should have been us.

"How are you feeling?" I asked as I grabbed a pair of gloves.

"I'm tired, hot and sweaty. I'm hoping for some good news," she moaned as she leaned into her husband's chest for support.

"This may be a little uncomfortable," I warned standing in front of her. "Can you lift your legs up for me?" She did so. I shook my head. "Only seven to eight," I said taking off my gloves and dropping them off in the hazard box.

"Ugh!" she moaned laying her head back on her pillow. "My head hurts," she said as she breathed deep. My heart went out to her as I watched her prepare for another contraction. Her husband Chris just like before was there to coach her through it. I want a love like that again. They seemed so happy and put together. They reminded me of Brandon and I. She's a English major and two semesters away from graduating, while he's a Architect who works for a company just outside of Annapolis. I documented her vitals. Her blood pressure was slightly elevated but nothing to be worried about.

"I say another hour or so." She nodded her head yes and then I left.

An hour passed and I just made my rounds. I was making my way to check on Gabby when her husband met me out in the hall way. By then Dr. Wadi was already in the room. It didn't take long for me to follow suit.

"What's going on?"

"She's not breathing," Dr. Wadi barked. "Oxygen now."

"You have to wait outside sir," Laura told Chris Gabby's husband.

Everything seemed to happen so fast. Time went by like a blur. We did all we could do, but we couldn't save Gabby or her baby. I don't know how it all went wrong but apparently the headache she had was the beginning of a stroke. By the time we got to the baby it was too late. Baby Lisa was called home with her mother. I couldn't even bring myself to look at her husband. I didn't have the energy to give my condolences for his loss.

The wounds from my parent's death still fresh I empathized with his moans of anguish that echoed through the hall way. His entire world has been turned upside down in one day. I had two hours left on my shift but my mind was all over the place and the charge nurse allowed me to leave. I could barely control my emotions as I made my exit. Bystanders and other employees throughout the hospital asked me if I was okay. I simply nodded my head yes and kept it moving. As soon as I hopped into my truck I placed my head on my steering wheel and balled like a new born baby. I cried for my sister, I cried for my parents, I cried for my own child that I never got a chance to meet, I cried for Chris, Gabby and baby Lisa. I cried so hard my head hurt. I released so much pent up anguish through my tears but it still did little to ease the pain I felt in my heart.

Savannah

I don't know how or why I ended up here but I did. He's the last person I should be running to but here I am five thirty in the morning taking refuge outside of his house. My nerves were calm as I stepped out of my truck and made my way up the steps. I looked from my right to my left, than I knocked and waited. A few minutes passed by, nothing happened so I knocked again.

I wrapped my lab coat around my body. A slight chill danced around as I continued to wait. It was still dark out but the sun looked like it would make an appearance at any minute. I started to knock again but I heard footsteps approaching.

"Who is it?" he snapped. Despite the irritation in his voice, my heart still skipped a beat. I took a deep breath and swallowed the lump in my throat.

"Savannah."

When he opened the door I swear I exhaled. He had the prettiest green eyes known to man. I could tell he was surprised to see me but that quickly turned to concern.

"Hey Savannah, is everything okay?" he asked peeking outside and looking around.

He was still dressed for bed wearing a pair of pajama pants and a wife beater. His biceps bulged out of his shirt and my mouth watered. I scanned over his body and bit my bottom lip. He's the true definition of God's gift to women. I responded by cupping his face and pressing my lips to his. His reaction is what I hoped for. He wrapped his arms around me and kissed me aggressively. But before I could take things a little further he pulled away from me.

"Savannah . . . wait!" he said. But I didn't want to wait. I needed this or maybe it was just an excuse to find my way back to him.

"Brandon please!"

He searched my eyes as I searched his. Without saying another word he scooped me up in his arms and carried me upstairs to the bedroom we once shared. My pussy was sloppy wet and my clit throbbed in anticipation. We broke free from our kiss as he laid me down on the bed. I watched as he took off his beater and slid out of his pants. I sent praises to the heavens as I stared at what the good man upstairs blessed him with. Just the sight alone had my box hot.

I couldn't resist as I sat up and took him in my mouth. I know what y'all thinking Savannah is a good girl and don't get down like that. Please, I get's down for my man, well for this man anyway. I relaxed my jaws and took all of what he had to offer. He hissed as I hummed and massaged his balls with my hand. I eased back and specifically gave the head of his dick my undivided attention. I circled the tip of his dick with my tongue as I looked up at him. The look on his face as he looked down at me was priceless.

He grabbed my shoulders as I grabbed the base of his dick with both hands and massaged it as I bobbed up and down on his anaconda. "Shit girl," he moaned biting his bottom lip. "Got dayum," he said taking me out of his mouth. "Hmmmm," he growled as he pushed me back on the bed and undressed me piece by piece until I was in my birthday suit.

All the bull shit that transpired between us I put to the back of my mind for now. I allowed him to caress my body with his fingers as he found a spot on my neck and lightly began to suck on it. I wrapped my arms around his neck and savored this moment. I got lost in the familiarity of his touch, his smell, it's a shame how much I still love this man.

"Brandon," I whispered when he inserted two fingers inside of my waterfall while he used his thumb to make circular motions around my clit. It didn't take long for my juices to gush out of me like a volcano. I didn't have a chance to recover before he placed himself in between my thighs.

He kept his eyes on me as he spread my pussy lips apart and tackled my clit like it was a quarterback and he was a linebacker. The shit he did with his tongue should be illegal. He licked, sucked and prodded me into submission. He held me hostage like he was punishing me for taking it away. He had my love box dripping and I was lying in puddle of the mess he created but I would be lying if I said I didn't enjoy it.

"Brandon, please," I begged trying to push him away. I couldn't take it anymore.

"Come mere," he said gripping my thighs and dragging me back towards his face. "I missed this pussy," he moaned. He forced two more orgasms out of me. "I missed you Savannah," he whispered as he made a trail of kisses along my stomach, until he reached the center of my chest. He stuck out his tongue making a trail until he reached my nipple.

He swallowed it in his mouth and I couldn't resist as a slight moan breezed through my lips. I grabbed the back of his head and closed my eyes as he did windmills around my nipples with his tongue. My pussy was on fire and I couldn't stand it. I needed to feel him. I grabbed his face and brought it to mine. I smothered my lips over his as he got comfortable in between my legs.

Inch by inch he placed himself inside my cave. I gasped and held on for dear life as he gently stretched my walls making room for his girth. I placed my face in his neck as our body's synchronized into a beautiful melody that only we could appreciate. He worked his pole around my walls like clock work, he was working overtime on this pussy and he damn near had me climbing the walls. I haven't had it this good in a long time and I wanted to make it last forever. I grabbed his ass and pushed him deeper inside of me.

"Got dayum, girl," he whispered into my ear. "I missed this baby girl. Damn I missed this shit," he said before gently biting my ear. "I love you Savannah."

"I love you too, Brandonnnnnnnnn," I screamed as I came. "Shit," I whimpered. He grunted and moaned into my ear until he reached his.

He lay on top of me out of breath. He balanced himself on his hands as he looked down at me. Tears glossed over his eyes, but I knew he would never allow them to fall. The love he held for me was still strong as ever. I could see it in his eyes. I cupped the back of his head and allowed his lips to greet mine. He kissed me with so much passion it scared me.

After we shared a moment he rolled over on the bed beside me and got comfortable. I placed my back into his chest, he placed his nose in my hair. I know he's confused about what just happened between us, shit I'm shocked by my own actions now that everything is said and done. Are me and Brandon officially back together no. Will we talk about this, definitely, just not right now. I needed something to take the edge off my emotional state of mind and he happened to be it.

I could feel my eyes getting heavy. I needed my rest to prepare me for the reality I had to face when I woke up. Maybe a nice get away would do me some good.

Brandon

I'm still trying to wrap my mind around what just went down between me and Savannah. I know we're trying to squash whatever beef or ill feelings we had between us but I never thought in a million years she would end up in my bed like this. As I looked down at her sleeping so peacefully beside me my heart begin to hurt. I don't deserve her and I realize that now.

She left me for whatever reason but I figured that's Karmas way of showing me how much a bitch she is, but hey I bought it on myself. I never should have cheated on her in the first place. I was drunk but I never should have gotten drunk to the point I couldn't control my actions. Being drunk wasn't an excuse and I can accept that. It's only right I tell Savannah the full story, she deserves to know.

When I told her I cheated on her she didn't ask a lot of questions which shocked me, but at the same time I wasn't forth coming with the information either. With so much shit going on in her life I knew now wouldn't be a good time but this was weighing ne down. I sighed as I looked up the ceiling. I wonder where things stand between us now. I glanced at the clock on my stand. It was a little past ten-thirty.

Savannah's phone has been blowing up non stop since she got here. I smirked because I had a feeling it was ole boy, Brian. I didn't even know she was in a relationship. It's none my business but damn I wondered how she managed to keep that shit under wraps. I ain't gone front I checked her social media profile through other people because she unfriended and blocked me. Not once did she ever change her relationship status. But he was the nigga by her side at the funeral. I could tell by the way he catered to her that he was her man.

That shit had me fucked up. I guess in the back of my mind I thought we would get pass whatever we were going through and get back together. So much for that shit. Savannah's a good girl and what I know of Brian the two just don't mix, but as long as he's treating her right and he don't put his hands on her we good. I want the best for her nothing less. I wonder where ole dude at anyway? Was he the reason she popped up at my door five o clock in the morning? Whatever the reason is I damn sure ain't complaining.

I leaned over kissed her forehead and carefully slid out of bed. I walked to my bathroom and relieved my bladder, brushed my teeth and took a quick shower. When I walked back out of the bathroom she was still sleeping so I figured the least I can do is make her some breakfast. I threw on a pair of boxers then headed to the kitchen battling with my thoughts and emotions. Fucking around with Savannah just took me two steps backwards.

"Damn," I said out loud to myself. I hope she don't have me out here stalking her ass again.

I fixed baby girl steak, eggs and grits. Yes ya boy can throw down. Shit I really ain't have a choice living with Savannah's non cooking ass. She tried on several occasions but when baby girl started burning simple shit like Ramen Noodles and hot dogs I knew it was time to let that dream go.

Savannah must have smelled what I was working with, because I walked back into the bedroom she was sitting up with the blanket wrapped tightly around her body. She smiled at me and started playing in her hair. I miss moments like this. I spoiled her ass and I wouldn't mind doing it again if she would let me, but I doubt I will ever get that chance again.

"Smells good," she smiled up at me.

"You know how I do," I said sitting the tray in front of her.

"Thank you."

"You're welcome. You know I'll do anything for you Savannah." She smiled and closed her eyes to say her grace. She must have been hungry because she didn't waste anytime going in. I thought the air around us would be a little tense but it wasn't. "So how you been?"

"Okay, I guess," she said shrugging her shoulders.

"You want to talk about it?"

"No, not really. I'm good."

"Are you sure? You know you can come to me about anything."

She looked at me long and hard. The pain I caused was still there, I can see it in her eyes. I didn't want to hurt her anymore than I already have, but it's some shit she needs to know. Once she finds out I know it will be the end of us, and I'm willing to accept that. I don't have a choice. I sensed she wanted to ask me something but she was holding back.

"Go ahead and say it," I coached her gently rubbing her arm. She shook her head no.

"I can't. I know we need to talk but I just can't handle anything else right now Brandon."

She was on the verge of tears and I ain't gone lie seeing her like that fucked with my heart. I hate seeing her upset. When she hurts I hurt.

"It's cool. Finish your food. You know ya greedy ass like to eat." That got a smile out of her.

"Negro please."

"Hey I'm just saying."

Silence fell between us and I found myself staring at her. Everything about her was still the same. She's still beautiful as ever. Damn how I wish I could turn back the hands of time. I fucked up. It wasn't a little fuck up either, but I fucked up big.

"I'm leaving town," she finally said out of the blue. I frowned.

"What?"

"I just need to get away. I need to clear my head."

"You can't up and run away when shit gets tough Savannah. Sometimes you have to face that battle head on and stand strong no matter the out come. You running to where ever isn't going to bring your parent's back."

"I know Brandon," she snapped. "I just need a vacation from everything and everyone. I just need peace of mind," she sighed.

She looked tired and worn out. I wonder what was really up but I had a feeling she wouldn't tell me. That's one thing I hated about Savannah. It's always a struggle to get her to open up and talk about her feelings. She likes to keep shit bottled up and that ain't healthy. I try to tell her she needs to let some of that stress out before she snap out and find herself confined to some crazy house.

I didn't want to press the issue then again I did. I hated that she refused to let me in as usual. Sometimes I just wanted to grab her and shake the hell out of her. I wanted to let her have a moment but I couldn't let this opportunity pass. She was here now so I had to ask.

"Why did you leave me?" I asked. She was about to put a piece of steak in her mouth but stopped. She placed her fork back on the tray.

"Are you serious?"

"Dead serious!"

"I don't want to talk about this right now."

"Why not? Oh I see, you just wanted to hit it and quit it. Huh?" She laughed and shook her head. "I don't see what's so damn funny Savannah. All this time I've been trying to reach out and see what's up and you straight dissed me. Wouldn't even give me the time of day. So now you here, get on your grown woman shit and tell me what's good."

"Okay Brandon," she said pushing her tray to the side. "You cheated on me muthafucka, that's what the fuck happened!" she snapped jabbing a finger in my forehead.

Damn I would pay to see the expression I had on my own face. I wasn't expecting her to come back at me like that and she put hands on me. That ain't Savannah. She must be going through something which I can understand. Her parents just died. I know I'm being selfish but I need answers.

"So you still tripping off shit I did years ago." She snapped her neck back and looked at me crazy. Her top lip curled and she rolled her eyes. "What?" I asked.

"So you gone sit there and front?" she asked.

Does she know, I wondered.

"You had some bitch up in my fucking house, where I lay my head at that's what's good."

"What!"

"I guess you ready to play dumb now huh?" she asked snaking her neck. "You wanted to have this conversation. You asked me muthafucka now you want to sit there and play like you don't know what the fuck I'm talking about."

"I don't."

"You know what . . . fuck this . . . ," she said taking what was left her food and throwing it across the room. "And fuck you," she shouted.

She stood up and let the blanket she had wrapped around her drop to the floor. For a moment I forgot about our conversation as I slowly scanned over her body. I licked my lips as my eyes traveled down to her shaved pussy. Visions of the love we made earlier flashed in my mind and my dick jumped against my thigh, but that flash back was short lived. I ducked just in time to miss the clock Savannah threw at me.

What the fuck," I said jumping up.

"I hate you," she screamed at me like she just didn't tell me she loved me a few hours ago. I ain't no punk but this is a side of Savannah I've never met. "I remained loyal to your monkey ass after you cheated the first time."

The first time? What the hell, she trippin, I thought to myself.

"But no, you couldn't keep your dirty dick in your pants, and then you had the nerve to disrespect me by bringing a bitch up in my house! OUR HOUSE!" She was all over the damn place. By now tears were falling from her eyes. "You ruined everything, you ruined me," she said pointing at her chest.

Seeing Savannah like this fucked with me heavy. I know I'm the cause of her emotional rollercoaster but right now baby girl was talking in circles. I only cheated on her once. I don't know where she getting that shit about me having some bitch up in here. I've done some fucked up shit but fucking another chick in our spot ain't it.

She's standing there looking at me with disappointment written on her face. My heart couldn't take it. I sighed and dragged my hands down the side of my face. I got up and walked over to her, that was a mistake. She cocked back and slapped the shit out of me. She hit me so hard spit flew out of my damn mouth. I don't hit women but got damn she had me seeing stars and I balled up my fist.

"Don't fucking touch me," she snapped. Her chest heaved up and down. She had this wild look in her eyes. She sat down on the bed and let out a gut wrenching cry that cut my soul.

"Savannah, I never meant to hurt you," I said kneeling down in front of her.

"But you did," she sniffled before wiping her face with the back of her hand. "You crushed me to the fucking core. I tried to get over you, but I can't," she sighed. "We were supposed to be a family. I never even got a chance to tell you about the baby."

"Baby? What baby."

"I was pregnant."

"Please don't tell me you killed my seed?" She shook her head no.

"I would never do that. I think it was the stress from a broken heart," she said finally looking at me. I got on my knees and took her hand in mine.

"Baby girl I swear on my life I only cheated that one time. I don't know what the fuck you talking about having some bitch up in here. You know I would never disrespect you like that," I pleaded as I swallowed the lump in my throat. I would eat my words later, but I needed to get to the bottom of this. She looked up at me with sad eyes.

Savannah

I know I probably look a hot mess, but I could care less right about now. I know my got damn hand hurts from slapping his ass, but that was long overdue. Now he up here looking me dead in the eye trying to lie his way out of the shit. Why couldn't he just be straight with me? He wanted to ask the million dollar question now he sitting here looking at me like I'm crazy and he don't know what the fuck I'm talking about.

This is why I need to get away, because I feel myself about to snap and bust a few heads open. I already stepped out of character by hitting his ass. That ain't me, I never resort to shit like that, but I couldn't hold back anymore. This rage just took over me and his face happened to be an outlet. It was time for me to get out of dodge. I couldn't stay here, it was just too much. I have more than enough money to take a long ass vacation and ya girl was about to do just that.

"I have to go," I said standing up searching the floor for my clothes. The reminder of what we did slid down my thighs. "This was a mistake," I said attempting to step around him but he placed his hands on my waist and held me in place. I looked down at his pathetic ass and rolled my eyes.

"Savannah I swear on my life, on my mother's life I have no idea what you are talking about. I only cheated once and I admit that shouldn't have happened. You can't leave me in the dark like this." The longer I stood there the more amped up I got.

"Move!" I snapped. He didn't move as quickly as I wanted him to but he eventually got the hint.

I left him standing there as I walked to the bathroom and relieved my bladder. I grabbed a rag, a bar of soap and turned on the shower. I hopped in and thought about my current situation. I don't know what the hell I was thinking. This was wrong on so many levels. Sleeping with Brandon is only making it harder for the old wounds to heal. I swear I do some of the dumbest shit.

The sincerity in Brandon's eyes was getting to me though. If he admitted to the first mistake why wouldn't he admit to the second? I thought about Zee and what she said about the facts not adding up. She's right Brandon wouldn't be dumb enough to have another chick up in my house knowing damn well that I was on my way home. Could it be that this all was a fucking set up? I groaned as I thought about it. I don't have the energy to deal with another headache right now. I'm too tired and drained to even cry. I looked over my life and thought about what could have been. Who the fuck is out to get me? Did this all tie into my parent's murder? Are people that desperate and crazy that they fuck with peoples lives like this? So many questions flew through my mind my head started to hurt.

Brandon was sitting on the bed when I stepped back into the bedroom. I wrapped the towel tighter around my body as I approached him. I knew he wanted to say something but I held up my hand.

"I believe you," I said. He clapped his hands together and smiled.

"Thank you. Now can you tell me what the fuck happened?"

"Yeah, but I need something to calm my nerves. Go fix me a drink."

"This early?"

"I really don't think I stuttered. Let's go," I said

"Where we going?"

To the bar," I simply said and walked out of the room leaving his ass sitting there.

*****

"Are you sure about this?" Brandon asked me as we pulled into the Hertrich car dealership.

"Yes, I know you want to get to the bottom of this, and I do to but right now just ain't the time. My heart just isn't in it."

I know that last line bruised his ego but every bit of it was the truth. I wanted answers as to who purposely tried to turn my life upside down but I wasn't in the right frame of mind to deal with extra bull shit. I just lost my parents and who knows whoever the bitch is could be right up under my damn nose. Besides I had to work on me first. Right now I'm too emotional and to vulnerable.

"So you just gonna up and leave? Just run away from shit?"

"Damn right. Somebody is gunning for me. I don't know who, or even why? I'm blind to everything going on around me. I'm not about to sit here and wait for whoever it is to come for me," I snapped. I need to get the hell out of dodge and lay low for a while until I figure something out."

"We can go to the police." I jerked my neck as I turned and looked at him. He deserved the eye roll I just gave him.

"Really Brandon! What the hell we gone say huh? That somebody drugged you over a year ago just so we could break up? Mind you, you don't even remember what happened."

"Fine fuck it. Carry your ole bull headed ass on to Georgia then."

"And don't tell anybody where I am," I warned pointing a finger at him as I got out of the car.

"Fine," he snapped back at me.

After our talk earlier that day we both still had a lot of unanswered questions but I wasn't about to stick around and find someone to answer them either. He couldn't understand where I was coming from. Somebody was after me and I ain't going to lie that shit had me shook. I couldn't go to the police with this bull shit they would look at me like I was crazy, so the best thing for me to do is get out of dodge. I made the necessary phone call to my job. Brandon said he would house sit for me while I stayed with my Aunt down in Georgia. She just remarried and told me I was more than welcome to come and visit. I'm definitely taking her up on her offer.

I tied up loose ends with the police department because I knew Brian, Roxie, and Zaheeda would come looking for me. I loved them all well except for Brian's crazy ass but I had to do what I had to do. The only person I trust at this point is Brandon. I know funny right. Hopefully I won't be down there long and somehow and someway some truth will come to the light.

"So you just gone dip out just like that huh?" Brandon asked me for the umpteenth time.

"Well, I still have a few things to take care of. I'm not vanishing completely. I'll be back. I still have to make my rounds and mail off a few letters." He nodded his head.

"Just be careful Savannah. Don't hesitate to call me if you need anything."

"Thanks," I smiled up at him.

I know this move was probably wrong on so many levels but I couldn't resist. Someone cheated us out of our happy ending, maybe there might be hope for us after all. I grabbed his hand and stood on my tippy toes. He met me half way. When our lips touched it was like magic. For a moment everything was forgotten. I pulled away and I was struck with my harsh reality.

"I love you Savannah."

"I love you too Brandon." He wiped away my tears.

"It's going to be okay. I promise," he said pinching my chin.

I nodded my head yes. I gave him a hug, and he damn near tried to squeeze the life out of me. I hopped in the brand new Toyota Camry I just purchased. It wasn't top notch but it would do until I safely made it to my destination. Yep I'm taking that long ass drive to Georgia. I think it will do me some good. I started up my car without looking back I peeled out of the parking lot and headed home. I still had a few loose ends to tie up before I made this long trip to the south.

Roxie

Something wasn't right I could feel it in my spirit. It wasn't Gabby, I guess she finally decided to rest her soul because she hasn't bothered me all night. I sat up and glanced at my clock it was a little after two in the afternoon. Today should be a workout day but I haven't been up to doing much because Gabby decided to pop up and temporary test my sanity. Hopefully she is behind me now and I can do something positive with myself.

Morning breath was heavy on my tongue and I wasn't feeling that. It was definitely time to get up and get my day started. I rolled over grabbed my phone off my stand and checked the usual, missed calls, text messages and Facebook. I had a few messages pop up in my inbox. I shook my head because thirsty niggas stayed in my inbox. Trust me when I say the thirst is real. These fuck boys need to realize it takes more than a nice sized dick to get close to a bad bitch like me. Besides you can't believe what dudes put in your inbox now in days, mess around and get cock fished.

I blame these insecure females for the actions of these so called men of today. They got these niggas thinking that a dinner at Chick Fila means we fucking by the end of the night. Tuh! Then they give away half of their taxes for five strokes of mediocre dick and five licks of the pussy. I laugh and shake my head at the foolery. How you go from being single all year and then income tax time you all of a sudden in a relationship. I need these desperate chicks and thirsty niggas to get they life.

Still checking through my messages I got up and headed to the bathroom. I had a message from Vee and my lips curled. Oh well she can wait. I placed my phone on the sink, took a piss and hopped in the shower. After my much needed shower I brushed my teeth, and pulled my long hair into a ponytail. I couldn't bypass my reflection without admiring it. Humph all I can say is the man upstairs created a God when he created me. Or is it Goddess? Whatever the hell it is all I can say is this chick right here is fiyah.

Green eyed, red bone with curves so steep a nigga might crash fucking with me.

People always ask me if I'm mixed with something. Who knows I could be. My mother was light skin, with long beautiful hair. I inherited my green eyes from her also. I can't even front my mother was beautiful, she just had a fucked up attitude. I guess it stems from her fucked up childhood. She would talk to me on occasions well more like she talked at me. She use to rant about how her mother didn't love her and treated her different because of the way she looked. She was the youngest of three and her mother had no idea who her daddy was.

I use to feel sorry for her then I stopped. Shit she wasn't doing anything for me anyway. She basically said fuck me and fed me to the damn wolves. That bitch never told me she loved me, never showed me any type of affection so any and everything she got she deserved it in my book. That includes my sorry ass excuse for a father. I shook my head because all this negative thinking is starting to slowly kill my vibe. I grabbed my phone still butter bald naked and walked into my bedroom. I grabbed the bottle of lotion that sat on my dresser as I unlocked my phone to read the message that Vee left me. As soon as I started reading my heart dropped to my stomach. The bottle of lotion I held in my hands fell to the floor.

Roxie,

Just figured I would let you know that I'm leaving town for a little while. I know it's a fucked up way to leave but I have a lot of shit I need to figure out. It's only a temporary thing I'll be back. Don't be mad, won't be gone long I promise. Love ya.

I snapped my neck back as I read the message she left me at least twenty times. I dialed her number and it went straight to voicemail. I know I called a good five more times but got the same damn result.

"Really Vee, you just gone up and leave like that without talking to me first? That's some punk ass shit and you know it. If you needed something you could have came to me instead of running away. Get on ya grown woman shit Vee," I shouted before ending the call.

As soon as I ended that call I called back and left another message. "Vee, I'm sorry I didn't mean to come at you like that. Please just call me and let me know that you are okay."

After I ended that call I got the urge to call her ass back and cuss her out but I didn't. I placed my phone on the bed beside me and ran my hand over my head. Did she really up and leave or was she on some bull shit? I looked at my phone and frowned, than I jumped off the bed and got dressed. I damn near broke my neck as I ran down the steps. I stepped outside only to realize I left my keys inside. I did a quick U turn grabbed my keys and hopped in my Range and headed over to Vee's house.

Her truck wasn't in the driveway. Any hope that she was just playing a joke instantly deflated. I parked my truck in the designated spot Vee would usually park hers and walked up to her front step and knocked on the door. This is ridiculous. Vee has me out here looking like a damn fool. I'm supposed to be her best friend and she ups and pulls this shit. This is tacky as hell and so damn high school. That bitch always preaching about me being so damn childish and immature but sending somebody a note on Facebook is the adult thing to do right, girl bye. She probably waltzed her happy ass down to Georgia but where ever the fuck she is I hope she finds her life or I just might end it if I find her.

I walked back to my truck and sat there for a minute contemplating my next move. I grabbed my phone and reread the message she left me. It was pathetic and I'm definitely in my feelings about it. My emotions had me all over the damn place. I'm mad, hurt, upset just one big ball of mess. Vee cut me deep on this one. I can't believe she just up and left me like that.

Frustrated I carried my ass back home. I called Vee's phone but it went straight to voice mail. I snatched the card that Detective Harley left on my front door and ripped it in half. I wish he would just leave me the hell alone. I'm already dealing with enough stress I don't need him to add to it. Damn I wish I had Zaheeda's number. I paced my living room floor trying to think. There isn't anybody I could think to call. Her Aunt Tammy use to live across the street from Mom Karen and Pop Gerald but she moved years ago and I never kept in contact with them. Tammy was a little to ghetto for me and her daughter Sabrina was too quiet. That chick was creepy.

My hands were tied. I walked into my living room and plopped down on the couch. She actually left. I can't believe it. Words can't begin to describe the feeling penetrating my heart right now. The tears rolled down my face without much effort. I sat back, grabbed a pillow and wallowed in my feelings. My phone vibrated on my hip and I jumped. I grabbed it neglecting the tears that continued to roll down my cheeks.

"Ugh!" I said out loud and rolled my eyes. I placed my phone on the stand.

It was Damon a nigga I fuck with from time to time. I think he is one of those down low brothers because most of the straight men I know ain't taking a dildo up the ass. But I guess because he's a lawyer and still enjoys the luxury of daddy's money he has to keep a certain image. So he's unhappily married with two children. After two more unanswered calls he sent me a text message. I sighed but got over my feelings for the time being because at the end of the day I knew I wanted that stack. I pretty much quit my day job as a medical assistant. It was just a front anyway. I can't wait for the day when Vee finally comes to her senses and we can be together like were meant to and I can leave this old life behind.

Damon: What's up
Me: Who this???
Damon: Oh, so it's like that now? It's me Damon
Me: Damon ???
Damon: Damn shawty, I know it's been a minute but I ain't think I slipped ya mind like that. How could you forget about a nigga like me? Damon West from East side lol.

I looked at my phone and shook my head. He didn't act, look or talk like the type to take it up the dookie shoot. I can't stand these down low men. This is just my opinion I don't believe in all that bisexual bullshit. You either straight or gay it's just that simple. I can't stand niggas that front like they want pussy when all along you secretly like what I like. Ugh! It's not fair to the women that waste time on their sorry ass. That's another reason why I think our black women are so miserable.

You spend years in a relationship wondering why he doesn't show you any kind of affection, possibly thinking maybe it's you when all along it's his confused, down low ass. Yeah society has made it hard for people to be themselves and express their sexuality but so what, life goes on get over it. If your gay be happy and fuck what every body else says that's all I'm saying.

Damon: Hello! You still don't remember me?

Me: Yeah, I do now. It's been awhile. I thought you forgot about me lol. What you been up to?

Damon: Nothing, working and trying to stay a float as usual. What about you?

Me: Same here.

Damon: Can we make arrangements to set something up.

Me: It's cool with me. I'm flexible. We have to work around your schedule not mine.

Damon: Aight I'm down in Miami right now. Won't be down here for long. I'll look you up when I get back.

Me: Awe shit. Must be nice.

Damon: Mainly business, but hopefully I can get a little fun while I'm down here. The wife and kids are with me.

Me: Oh tell wifey I said hello.

Damon: You got jokes. Aight ma, I'll be in touch.

Me: Okay you do that.

Still no word from Vee and that shit pissed me off. I logged onto Facebook and checked out her page nothing, bland just like her cooking. I had to get up, get out and do something. This was still too fresh and I knew if I stayed in one spot I was bound to snap. I don't know where I'm going but I have to get the hell out of here. Even though Prince has been showing his ass lately I hit him up.

"Yeah," he answered like he was annoyed. I frowned temporarily taking the phone away from my ear and looking at it. I placed it back to my ear and smacked my lips.

"Well, hello to you too?" I snapped. I heard him sigh.

"What's up Roxie?"

"I'm trying to figure out the same thing."

"I just got a lot on my mind."

"And I don't. I just lost my parents."

"They weren't your real parent's Roxie."

I know he didn't. I counted down from ten in my head. My heart was racing and I was about to go in full bitch mode. Where is Prince and who is the bitch made nigga that he has suddenly been replaced with. I'm not use to being on the other side of the fence. Lately I've been the one doing all the calling, sending text messages, and leaving voicemails. Something's wrong with this picture.

"Really Prince? They raised me like I was their own and for you to come at me like that is some straight bull shit."

"You know what baby girl you right, my bad. I ain't feeling good today. Ace and Brian decided to go to Miami without me. I'm just in a fucked up state of mind right now. It's no excuse and I shouldn't be taking it out on you."

Why am I still wasting my time on this dude? Originally he was a way for me to get to Brian but that was an epic fail. At first he was all for the plan I mapped out for him then out of no where he decides to get a conscious. I had to see where his head is at though. That's all the fuck I need is for him to go back running his mouth.

"You want me to come over?"

"No, I'm good," he blurted out quickly. Too quickly.

My woman's intuition immediately kicked in. I frowned as I tried to think back when the last time we had sex. Come to think of it he hasn't tagged this pussy in a minute and hasn't even made an effort to. It's no secret I do my thing from time to time, I ain't pressed for dick it's just the principle. Don't make me into a side bitch without my permission. I pinched the bridge of my nose.

"Okay baby, I'll let you get some rest. I'll call you tomorrow and we can talk about it."

"Sounds good," he yawned. I rolled my eyes because I knew that shit was fake and all for show. It's all good though because best believe I got something in store for that ass. Men are so dumb, because I bet my last dollar that a bitch is laid up in his house right now.

"Feel better babe, love you."

"I . . . I . . . love you too," he hung up.

I fell out laughing. That's what he gets. I hope I'm wrong about this feeling that I have but I doubt it. When I have my suspicion about something I'm usually right, and I plan on finding out tonight.

Bri

Something's up with this dude because I've been going in on this dick for the past ten minutes and it still hasn't reached it's full potential. I let his dick slide out of my mouth and looked up at him. Just like I suspected his mind wasn't in it. I rolled my eyes and wiped my mouth with the back of my hand. Bae is out of town and I'm horny as fuck and this nigga up here wasting my damn time, it's all good because no doubt he will break me off with some bread. That's the only reason I fuck with his ass anyway. He's cute but he has no swag, so basically he's a cornball but his money makes up for that.

I sighed letting him know I was frustrated as I got up and sat beside him. He still didn't acknowledge me just continued to stare off at nothing. I frowned, because I could have stayed my black ass home or carried my ass down to Crazy Eight's for all this bullshit. Besides Prince has been tripping for the past couple of days and it's starting to make a chick feel a little uneasy. I really think he's fucking with his nose. The other night he had some white stuff around the bridge of his nose. When I questioned him about it he gave me some line about eating a powdered donut. Okay he should have slapped the stupid sign on my forehead if he thought I was falling for that. I checked my watch it was a little past nine. If I wanted I could still make it to Crazy Eights.

Crazy Eights is a strip club. It's okay. Nothing like the money I made in Baltimore. I miss the fast life up there and as soon as I get a chance I'm going back. Just need a little more time and hopefully shit smoothes over. It's no secret I'm a hoe. I made a name for myself while I was up there, jumping from one man to the next always on the search for a nigga with pockets deeper than my pussy. All was good until a scorned wife had her son ransack my home and I was forced to find my way back to the Lower Eastern Shore.

It's not so bad, but it could be better. In the beginning shit was rough and I was throwing more pussy than a fake bitch threw shade. Money was good too but I had to slow my roll a little after catching Gonorrhea. Ugh! The flash backs of that shit is so nasty. It's not my first STD but I plan on making sure it's my last, so I *try* to be more precautious.

I sat back and thought about bae. It's nothing serious, well at least not yet. I met his fine ass while working one night at Crazy Eights. I guess he liked what he saw because by the end of the night we were going half on a baby. He reminds me of the actor Morris Chestnut and the dick will have a bitch going in circles. He and his brother own a popular night club but I know for a fact that he does a few extracurricular activities that are illegal. That ain't none of my business as long as he keeps me stacked I'm good.

"I'm sorry baby," Prince finally decides to say to me as he gently squeezes my thigh.

"It's okay," I half smile and look at him. "Is everything good with you?" I turned my body towards him and gently caress his ear. I could tell by his facial expression that he wanted to tell me something but he was hesitant. "You can tell me," I cooed. "Your secret is safe with me."

"I got a lot of shit I'm dealing with right now," Prince said to me as he stuffed his dick back inside his boxers.

"We got all night," I said grabbing his remote control and turning the volume down on the TV. I had a feeling this was going to be juicy.

"I got a situation involving your girl."

"Who . . . Roxie?" I frowned because that's the only girl I really fucked with.

"Yeah."

"What about her?"

"She's crazy!"

I nodded my head in agreement. Roxie is a little off and I ain't gone front it scares me to think what she might do if she ever found out about us. I thought about my car sitting outside. That was reckless because usually he picks me up and drops me off but lately we've been careless. We're asking to get caught.

Besides Prince been throwing her a lot of shade so I know she suspects something. Men are so damn dumb. When you change your routine and start acting different women know. He pretty much stopped calling her, texting her, all of that above. He always talking that shit about us being together, but it ain't happening. He and I are just a temporary thing. The dick is good, the money is even better but that's about it. He's too soft for me. We haven't been fucking around that long and he was already in love.

Prince and I actually didn't get a formal introduction until the day of Savannah's parent's funeral. That's fucked up on so many levels but I couldn't help it. Like I said he's cute, but his diamonds made my pussy wet. I gave him a suggestive nod, despite the risks and he took the bait. We've been kicking it since. Besides I caught him eyeing my curves in the dress I wore at the funeral. Hell even the Pastor had to do a double take.

"We should tell her," he said looking over at me, with love in his eyes. It took everything within me not to frown. I needed him to get back to what he wanted to tell me.

"Didn't you just say she was crazy?" I asked.

"Yeah," he laughed. "She almost got me though."

"How?"

"You know she don't like my brother right." I nodded my head yes because that's no secret. Roxie can't stand Brian but it has a lot to do with Savannah. "Well, you know I want my own club and shit. So she concocted this plan on how I could do it. First she told me I had to get rid of Ace, frame Brian for the murder and while he's in jail he wouldn't have a choice but to hand the club over to me."

My mouth dropped and my heart started beating at my chest. I always knew Roxie had more than a few screws loose. She went through extreme lengths just to break up Brandon and Savannah but I never thought she would resort to murder. I definitely couldn't let that happen because Ace is my bae. I know what you're thinking that I'm fucking in circles and you're right.

"You're not going to do it are you?" I already knew the answer to that. He ain't about that life.

"Naw! I don't like that nigga, but I couldn't see myself killing him either. I want a club and all but betraying my brother like that to get it just ain't worth it." I was glad to hear that.

"Have you told Brian yet?"

"No. I've been sitting on this shit for a minute and I don't know how he's going to react. He ain't working with a full deck either."

"Why you say that?" I laughed, hoping he would take things a little further. I heard he killed his ex girlfriend Macy and her brother. I wonder if it's true.

"Cause he ain't. That nigga be talking to his self and shit."

"So, what's wrong with that? I talk to myself all the time."

"Do you answer yourself?"

"Sometimes." That made him smile.

"I love my brother man, but he's done some fucked up shit to innocent people." I remained quiet damn near on the edge of my seat, but nothing prepared me for what he was about to tell me. He sighed and stared at nothing in particular before he finally said it. "He killed Savannah's parents."

In the blink of an eye shit just got real. My heart literally dropped to my stomach and my mouth was wide open. I mean I'm shocked but than again I'm not. I could have sworn Brian had a smirk on his face when Savannah's parents were laid to rest. I tried to chalk it up as my imagination but after what Prince just told me I know it wasn't all in my mind.

"Damn," is all I can say. I wonder what the hell Savannah doing to make the muthafucka's around her go crazy. She's a pretty girl, but she ain't a bad bitch like me but she got nigga's out here killing to be with her. I can handle a lot of shit but this was a little more than I expected.

"I heard him and Ace talking about it," Prince said shaking his head. "I know Brian is knee deep in the streets and sometimes you have to go hard in his profession but he's a stone cold killer. He has no remorse about the shit. I ain't gone lie it's fucking with me. Savannah was broken up about her parent's man. They didn't deserve that, and Savannah didn't either."

I gave Prince a shoulder to lean on. He talked my damn ear off. I was glad when he finally carried his ass to sleep, but not before he dropped a stack on me. It was only ten thirty and in my eyes the night was still young. Even though he laid some bread on me I figured I could still stop by Crazy Eight's and make a little extra change. I looked over at Prince who was knocked out. I frowned at the dab of snot lingering outside of his nose. Yeah he's definitely on that bag. I quietly put on my shoes, grabbed my coat and made my exit.

The air was chilly as I stepped outside and I rubbed my arms a little. I pulled out my phone and scrolled through my missed calls as I headed towards my car. None of them were from Ace and I was in my feelings a little, but it alls good as long as I'm the first bitch he contact when he steps foot in Maryland then I'm straight. The health department called me too. I guess they finally got my test results. I was so into my phone I didn't even see her crazy ass coming but I felt the hard blow she landed upside my damn head. It didn't take much for her to knock me on my ass.

"You loose pussy bitch," she yelled at me. I tried to defend myself but it was no use. She was like a caged animal and she was letting loose on my ass.

"Roxie, get the fuck off me," I screamed as I some how managed to get a hold of her hair. I yanked hard on it, hoping it would give me some leverage or temporarily stop her from beating my ass, but that shit back fired because she came at me even harder.

"Fuck you. I should have never trusted your ass. I welcomed you up in my home and you up here fucking my man. You need to learn how to keep your pussy to yourself, yelp you gone learn today bitch," she said cocking me cold in the mouth.

Damn I really felt that one. My head went flying backwards and I hit the pavement. Immediately I began to see stars. I was in a dangerous territory because I was flat on my back. She looked down at me with this look in her eyes and my heart skipped a beat. My eyes slowly looked from side to side, there was no calling for help it was just me and her. I knew I fucked up big time. She stood over me and smacked the shit out of me.

"I don't even know what the fuck he sees in you. Bitch you probably ain't got no damn walls. If Waka Flaka made a song about no walls you'd be headlining that bitch." She brought her foot up and slammed it into my stomach.

"Ugh!" I gasped. "Roxie, please." Ain't this some pathetic shit though? Word of advice if you plan on being a side chick please learn how to fight, carry some mace, something. The money is good but I'm too old to be going through this shit. She kicked me and I could have sworn she broke a rib. "Roxie."

"That's my name bitch," she snapped, then kicked the shit out of me.

She plopped down on my chest, and I grunted. I was having trouble catching my breath. She grabbed my head and slammed it into the ground. Damn was he worth all this. I could have sworn she didn't want his ass, but that can wait later. The matter at hand is this bitch is trying to kill me.

"Roxie . . . wait . . .," I couldn't even defend myself if I wanted to. She had my arms pinned down at my sides. She gave me this cold stare and I almost pissed myself. "I know who killed Savannah's parents," I panted out of breath. This bitch wasn't playing she had all her weight on me.

"What?" she squinted.

"I said I know who killed Savannah's parents." I'm selling my soul to the devil, but I believe if she slammed my head down one more time on this pavement my ass would be grass. She looked at me like she didn't believe me.

"Who?"

"Brian!"

Roxie

Did she say what I think she just said? My heart was already racing from beating her ass now it seemed like it was going a mile a minute. I couldn't even move as I looked down at Bri. Damn I fucked her ass up good. Her eye was swollen, both her nose and lip was busted. She shouldn't have slept with my damn man. I swear chicks now days are scandalous. All I can do is shake my head. How you gone take on the roll of a side chick and can't fight. If that's the career path you choose the number one qualification should be to know how to throw them bows.

"Roxie."

I cut my eyes at her. She was scared but I don't give two shits. She sure as hell didn't show me no mercy when she was on my man's dick so why should I show her any. If it weren't for the information she just told me I swear this pavement would be painted with her blood. For her sake I hope she ain't lying or that's definitely her ass. I smacked her one more good time and hogged spit on her as I stood up.

"Get up, "I snapped.

"Ugh!" she groaned in pain but I was unmoved.

Thinking about how she stayed up in my home had me in my feelings. I started to hit her again, just for that but I had other things to worry about. I hope what she just said about Brian wasn't true but I could see him doing some fucked up shit like that. What I don't like is the cops hounding me like I had something to do with it. I bet his crazy ass sitting back laughing at me. My mind shifted to Savannah and I wondered if the message she sent me on Facebook was real.

Twenty minutes later we were sitting in my kitchen. I sipped on my Moscato as I shook my head at Bri's pitiful ass. I swear this bitch is weak. If I were her as soon as I hit my car I would have gotten the hell out of dodge but I guess I had her ass shook because here she is sitting in my kitchen telling me her story of how she and Prince made googlie eyes at Mom Karen and

Pop Gerald's funeral. That's ratchet. Another shocker was hearing that she's fucking with Ace, I ain't gone lie I was in my feelings about that one. He was one nigga that could get it but Prince ruined that for me, but that's okay. I got something for his ass and Brian too. He gone regret the day he became my best friends man.

"Roxie, I'm so sorry," Bri started.

"Save it," I said holding up my hand. She flinched and I smirked. "You better not be lying to me Bri."

"I swear on my life, that's what he said. He even said he stopped fucking with you like that because you wanted him to kill Ace, blame Brian and that way he could take over Brian's club."

Prince was running his lips and that shit could be hazardous. I'm betting he hasn't told Brian yet, so I had to put some shit in motion and quick.

"Brian and Ace are still in Miami right?"

"Yeah, Why?" I cut my eyes at her like she was crazy for questioning me. "Sorry," she whispered and lowered her eyes.

I never thought Bri was this soft. I got up and left her sitting there. I went into my bedroom and made a phone call. It was early in morning but I really didn't care.

"Hello." As soon as he answered I decided to skip the pleasantries.

"Do you know where Savannah is?"

"Roxie! What the hell? Do you know what time it is?"

"Yes, now answer the damn question." There was a slight pause. "Please, Brandon I'm just worried about her that's all." He sighed.

"No, I don't know where she is but I do know that she's okay."

I knew he was lying but as long as she's okay I will worry about her location later. But if Savannah was reaching out to Brandon then I had a new set of problems on my hands. All I need is for them to get close and for him spill our secret. I love Savannah to much to allow that to happen.

"If you talk to her please just tell her to call me," I whispered. It hurt like hell that Vee up and left the way she did. No phone call, nothing like I didn't mean shit to her. Like our friendship didn't mean anything.

"Okay Roxie."

"You didn't say anything did you?" I asked after a brief moment of silence.

"No!"

"Good, make sure it stays that way," I said and hung up without giving him a chance to respond. I went back down stairs and Bri was still sitting at the table with an ice pack on her eye. "You can go now," I sighed. She looked at me.

"Are you still mad at me Roxie?"

"You damn right I am. I gave your ass a place to stay all the while you checking out my man."

"I'm sorry," she whined.

"Bri, just leave please."

I had a lot of shit on my mind and her being there put me on edge. I needed to sort some things out. I don't know how long Savannah planned on staying away but I wanted Brian well out of the picture before she got back. Bri nodded her head and simply got up and left. If she's smart she will keep her mouth shut and stay away from Prince. I think the ass whooping I gave her should be convincing enough. As soon as I turned around guess who decides to make a grand appearance. I damn near jumped out of my skin as I placed my hand over my chest. I rolled my eyes wishing I could wipe that damn smirk off her face.

"What the fuck do you want Gabby?"

"It's all going to be over soon."

"Shut the fuck up," I snapped at her as I made my way upstairs. There was no way I could think at my best with her here fucking up my vibe.

"It is and it's going to end bad. You've been warned."

I turned around to give that cold bitch a piece of my mind but she was gone. She had me so heated I was sweating. Something had to give I can't keep living like this.

Brian

Two damn weeks and not even so much as a kiss my ass from Savannah. I wanted to give her the benefit of the doubt so I gave her, her space. I don't think she meant what she said about ending this relationship. I think she was just stressed out about her parents at least that's what I've been telling myself. I needed someone to keep my mind occupied while I was down in Miami so I called crazy ass Melinda and she couldn't even do the trick. She nagged to damn much and she was possessive and jealous. I had to rough her ass up a little bit because she one of those bitches that don't know how to keep her hands to herself.

I couldn't even concentrate on anything else because as hard as I tried I couldn't keep Savannah off my mind. I even slipped up while me and Melinda were having sex and called Savannah's name. She smacked the shit out of me for that. Even though I was in the wrong I couldn't let her get away with putting her hands on me. I felt bad though because I pretty much left everything concerning our club up to Ace. I mean I was there but then I again I wasn't. My mind wasn't.

Savannah wasn't home when I pulled up and for the past hour I've been getting her voicemail. The shit pissed me off. My thoughts turned dark at the thought of her being with another man. I didn't hesitate as I used my key to allow myself to enter. As soon as I opened the door her alarm went off.

"What the fuck?" I panicked and looked around. This is weird because Savannah rarely uses it. I stared at the box because I don't know the code. "Fuck," I said out loud as I ran my hand over my head. I locked the door and got the hell out of dodge. I didn't know what else to do.

I carried my ass home mad as fuck because I still couldn't get a hold of Savannah. I hadn't been home a good five minutes before my neighbor Ms. Givens came sauntering over with a bag full of my mail. She must have been staking out the place.

"Did you enjoy your trip?" she asked me.

"Yeah," I said shortly grabbing the bag of mail out of her hands. I reached for my wallet but she stopped me.

"You don't have to pay me?" she said looking me dead in my eyes giving me that look.

I gave her the once over. She was easy on the eyes but she was old as hell. I know she had to be pushing about sixty. As good as she looked for her age I couldn't bring myself to go there. She had perfect caramel skin, and bright brown eyes. Her hair was pulled tight into a bun that sat on top of her head. She was dressed down today in a pair of leggings and a sweatshirt. Her thighs were toned and she had just enough ass to make me do a double take, but she was old enough to be my mother. Halle Berry would be the only exception I make concerning age.

"I don't mind," I said pulling out my wallet and handing her three one hundred dollar bills.

I shook my head as I sent her home with her tail in between her legs. I unlocked my door and walked in. I punched in the code on my alarm and headed straight upstairs. I had to get out of these clothes and take a shower. The plane ride wasn't bad but my body screamed at me to take a nap but I couldn't. I still hadn't heard from Savannah. She knew I was due back this weekend. Damn I thought she would at least be waiting on me since I haven't heard from her black ass.

"She was serious Brian. She said she can't do it anymore."

"No," I said shaking my head refusing to believe Savannah really didn't want me.

I called her again but received her voicemail. I don't have Roxie's number and she doesn't really have any friends locally besides that Zaheeda bitch. But I can' stand her ass either. They don't know but I doubled back on their ass that day both she and Roxie came over. She was talking real reckless about me like she knew me. Savannah was pissed about me trying to move in with her. She thought I over stepped my boundaries but she's forcing my hand. I'm trying to move forward with my life and I want her apart of it but she was making it harder and harder. Besides the deal didn't go through anyway. It just put me back at square one.

I stripped down to my birthday suit and walked into my bathroom. I didn't even wait for the water to get warm before I hopped in. I needed to wash my stress away. This relationship thing was driving me crazy. Why couldn't Savannah just do what I wanted, how I wanted and when I wanted? Thinking about her got my heart pumping again. I turned off the shower stepped out, grabbed a towel and wrapped it around my waist. I put some lotion on my body and threw on a pair of sweat pants and a shirt. I sat down on my bed and grabbed my phone.

Nothing! I swear it feels like somebody punched me in my damn chest. Fatigue was starting to set in and I knew I wouldn't be any good until I got some sleep. It was obvious the signs have been there all along. The voices in my head were right. Savannah doesn't love me, she never did and I know that she never will. I lay back on my bed, suppressing the tears of a broken heart. Imagine that. As heartless as I am when it comes to killing a nigga, I'm up here crying over some bitch.

*****

After my nap I got up, checked my phone and still nothing. By now the hurt I felt before had been replaced with anger. I got up grabbed my keys, jumped in my car and headed straight to her house. Car horns beeped at me left and right but I didn't care. I was on a mission. When I pulled up to her house I was heated.

I didn't even bother to knock I used my key and walked right up in that muthafucka like I owned it.

"Savannah!" I yelled walking into her living room looking around. I didn't even wait for a response as I entered the kitchen. This bitch was sitting at the table with her kindle in hand drinking a glass of wine. I frowned. "What the fuck?" I walked up on her. She must've of picked up on the hostility in my voice.

"What's wrong?" she had the nerve to ask me.

I could feel the veins popping out of my damn neck. We haven't spoken in damn near two weeks and she up here asking me what's wrong. My hands started to twitch. Visions of me wrapping my hands around her throat flashed in my mind.

"Brian, what are you doing here?" she asked with an attitude

"Huh!" I said confused.

"I guess we need to have this discussion again."

"Discussion about what?"

"Us," she said placing her kindle and glass of wine down on the kitchen table. I could tell by her sudden change of attitude that shit was about to get real. I know in my heart what she's about to say but I don't want to hear it. I didn't give her a chance to say anything. I reached out and wrapped my hands around her throat. Her eyes bucked in surprise. "Brian!" she clawed at my hands, my face, anything she could get her hands on but I was determined. The chair she sat in shifted under her weight but I still managed to hold her in place.

"It ain't over until I say it's over," I growled at her. She tried but she was slowly losing this battle. Her attempt to live had become feeble. A tear slid down my cheek. I kissed her forehead. "I love you Savannah," I whispered in her ear just before I snapped her neck.

I jumped up drenched in sweat. My head jerked from side to side as I adjusted my eyes to my surroundings. My heart pounded at my chest and my whole body was shaking. It was just a dream but damn it felt so real. I rubbed the back of my neck as I glanced at the clock on my stand. It was nine o'clock. If Savannah was working I know she had to be home by now. I checked my phone and still nothing from Savannah. I called her number and once again I was directed to voicemail. Now I started to worry. What if something happened to my baby? I stood up and paced my floor.

"Think Brian." I said out loud to myself. I snapped my fingers and then I called Prince.

"What's up B?" he answered. He didn't sound like himself but I had other things to worry about.

"What's Roxie's number?"

"Huh!"

"Nigga you heard me. I didn't stutter, now run the digits muthafucka." Damn I hate when people question me. I'm already aggravated and shit. He did as he was told and without hesitation I called her ass. She didn't answer until after the fifth time I called.

"Hello!" she snapped.

"Where's Savannah?"

"Who the fuck is this?"

"Its Brian, now where's Savannah?" There was a moment of silence and I thought she might have hung up so I took the phone away from my ear. The timer was still running so I knew she was still there. "Roxie!"

"I don't know," she calmly said, but I knew her ass was lying because she was too calm.

"Don't fuck with me Roxie," I snapped. She sighed.

"Brian, I don't know where Savannah is and playboy I haven't started fucking with you yet?"

"What?" I asked. I could feel the hard frown invade my forehead. "Look I don't have time to play these childish ass games with you Roxie. Just tell me where the fuck Savannah is!"

"Did anyone ever tell you that you catch more bees with honey?" she asked. I smirked and breathed deep.

"Can you please tell me where Savannah is?"

"I don't know."

"Roxie I -,"

"I don't know where the fuck she is. She just left."

"Huh! What the fuck you mean she left?"

"Just what the fuck it means. She left? She didn't tell you?" she asked me.

I picked up on the sarcasm in her voice. I knew that bitch was grinning from ear to ear. I sucked my teeth and hung up on her ass. My anger got the best of me and before I knew it I threw my phone across the room. I didn't see it hit the wall but I heard it. I whipped around and took my frustrations out on my bathroom door. I got at least two good licks in before a mind blowing pain shot through my hand and traveled up my arm.

"Awe shit," I cursed gripping my hand. Blood leaked through the cracks of my fingers and onto my carpet. "Fuck," I growled, as I walked into my bathroom in search of a towel. I found one and gently wrapped it around my wounded hand.

I didn't want to go the hospital because I knew they would ask a whole bunch of unnecessary questions that I'm not really in the mood to answer but I knew I had too. The pain was starting to get to me already. I could feel a headache ready to make an appearance. I walked back into the bedroom and the bag of mail caught my eye. I grabbed it as I walked down stairs and grabbed my keys.

There was no way I could drive like this. I grabbed my house phone and dialed Ace's number, but he wasn't answering his phone. Guess he still in his feelings about my lack of participation in Miami. Next I tried Prince but he wasn't answering either. Damn it's fucked up how you always there for somebody when they need you but when you need them they are no where to be found. I sighed because I didn't want to call her but I did. This bitch didn't waste no time answering the phone.

"Hey can you come get me?"

"What's wrong?" she asked. I could hear the concern in her voice but I wasn't in the mood to explain this sad story over the phone. I was starting to get agitated my hand hurt so damn bad.

"Melinda, just get over here damn!"

"Excuse the piss right out of me then. Where the fuck you at?"

"I'm at home, shit."

"Like I know where the fuck you live?" she said sucking her teeth. Damn she had a point. I never revealed where I really laid my head at. I didn't want to either but if I didn't get help for this shit and quick I was bound to snap. I quickly rattled off my address. "On my way Papi," she said then hung up.

It wasn't as bad as I thought. I managed to sprain both my hand and wrist. In the process of banging on the door I cut myself and had to get a few stitches. They gave me some pain medication, bandaged me up and told me to keep a cold compress on it periodically for the next couple of days. I told Melinda she could stay in the car but she had to bring her crazy ass inside. I had to check her a couple of times because she swore up and down that the x-ray tech tried to slip me her number. Well she did but I wasn't about to tell her crazy ass that.

I was just discharged; Me and Melinda were on our way to the car. Melinda was talking about something but I couldn't even fake like I was interested in the conversation. As crazy as it is my mind was still on Savannah. I still had the bag of mail that I hadn't had a chance to read yet. Something told me I would get some answers there.

"Hi Brian." Both Melinda and I stopped. I turned around and smirked. Just my luck!

"Sup," I said. Melinda picked up on my attitude. Once she realized Zaheeda wasn't a threat she relaxed.

"What happened to your hand?" she asked me all the while keeping her eyes trained on Melinda. I knew she was looking for a formal introduction but I wasn't giving her one. I don't owe her anything, she's Savannah's friend not mine. Well I hadn't planned on it but Melinda couldn't keep her mouth to herself.

"Hi, I'm Melinda," she said sticking her hand out. "You are?"

"Zaheeda."

"Zaheeda, I like it. What is that Swahili?" Melinda asked. I smirked and shook my head.

"No," Zaheeda simply answered. "Have you heard from Savannah?" she asked directing her attention back to me.

"Who the fuck is Savannah?" Melinda snapped placing her hands on her hips.

"His *girlfriend*," Zaheeda answered for me.

"You trippin' I already told you that," I snapped as I looked at Melinda sideways. Damn she lucky we in public or I would have slapped taste out of her damn mouth. Melinda is cool but she has the tendency to bring out the worst in me. I try to keep my hands to myself but she made it hard. Especially when she gets out of pocket. "I haven't heard from her. I don't even know what the fuck is going on," I confessed. She sighed.

"Well she sent me a message on Facebook saying she needed a break. Said she was going away. Didn't tell me where or how long? I spoke with my boss earlier and she said Savannah basically quit her job."

Damn, so it's official. She really up and left like that. She was serious about what she said but I still refused to believe it. My mind raced with so many questions but the person who had the answers was no where to be found. That was a bitch move, and I was determined to find her ass.

"She didn't tell you she was leaving?" Zaheeda asked pulling me out of my thoughts. My silence confirmed what she already knew. I guess she took that as initiative to talk about me and Savannah's relationship. "Maybe this is a sign."

"A sign of what?"

"Savannah's not happy," she said shrugging her shoulders.

"I mean she just lost her parents who would be happy about that?" I answered curling up my top lip. She breathed deep.

"I *mean* she's not happy with you. She's not happy with the *relationship.*"

"Bitch, you-,"

"Bitch," she snapped at me placing her hand on her hip. "I got ya bitch," she said taking a step towards me.

"Don't worry about me and Savannah and what we got going on, we good," I said taking a few steps of my own.

"Apparently not," she said rolling her neck and sucking her teeth. "She doesn't love you, doesn't want to be with you. She thinks your pushy, annoying and over bearing. Besides what grown woman wants to play with a fun sized penis?"

Before I had chance to react Melinda handled that mouthy bitch. She punched her so hard, she went flying back wards. I heard someone yell security. I grabbed Melinda's hand and calmly proceeded towards the exit. Damn I hated that I allowed that bitch to get under my skin. I can be a hot head at times but now wasn't the time or place for that shit. Melinda was hype but I quickly calmed her ass down because I needed to think. I didn't want to go straight home just in case that Zaheeda bitch ran her mouth and the cops decided to come looking for me.

"Nigga you getting soft." I tried to ignore the voice in my head but it kept coming. "These bitches got you out here looking like a fool. Savannah included. Fun sized penis, that's funny."

"Shut up!" I yelled placing my fingertips to my temples. My mind was racing and on top of the pain in my hand I couldn't think straight. I could see Melinda stealing glances at me but I shrugged it off.

"She can get it too," the voice said.

"Exactly what I was thinking," I mumbled under my breath.

Brian

Brian,

I hope this letter finds you in good health and I hope you enjoyed your stay down in Miami. I'm just sending this because I've decided to leave Maryland, just to clear my head. I know you wanted to continue the discussion we had the night before you left and my decision still remains the same. Take care.

Savannah.

I read that corny ass letter at least twenty five times. I'm still in that *wow* moment. Did she really try to play me like that in a fucking letter? I laugh out loud and shake my head. This is coming from a woman who talks about her best friend being so damn childish and how she needs to grow up but she turns around and dumps me in a damn letter. I crumbled it up with my good hand and threw it. I didn't even check to see where it landed.

Savannah got the game all fucked up if she thinks this is acceptable. I couldn't even control the anger that brewed in my chest add the pain, its like dark and white liquor it just don't mix. I couldn't control myself as I went to work on Melinda's kitchen. Within mere minutes it looked like a tornado went through it. I didn't even realize she'd come downstairs until I felt her go upside my damn head.

"Brian, what the fuck is wrong with you? STOP IT!" she screamed at the top of her lungs.

She slapped me so hard spit flew out of my mouth. After she hit me a nigga was seeing red. I forgot about my hand and punched her dead in the face. We both doubled over in pain. My hand hurt so bad my eyes began to water.

"Fuck!" I growled. I clenched my teeth, closed my eyes and waited for the throbbing to stop. It didn't completely stop but after a few minutes it eventually let up. I looked over at Melinda. She was holding her face staring at me with death in her eyes. "I'm a need you to fix your face ma."

"Fuck you!" she snapped as she carefully stepped through the mess I made. She grabbed a zip loc bag, put some ice in it and held it against her face. Her eye was starting to swell. "You can't stay here acting like this. You gotta go."

"I'll leave when I'm ready. You know better than to talk to me like that Melinda. Be ready in ten minutes I need you to take me somewhere.

"Where the fuck we going this time of night?" she snapped at me adding in an eye roll. I chuckled a little bit. I decided to let her attitude slide since I did just fuck up her kitchen. "I have to go to work."

"Just be ready in ten minutes."

She didn't respond simply mumbled something under her breath that I couldn't make out but I let it go. Forty-five minutes later we were sitting outside of my father's estate. We'd been here a good ten minutes waiting for him to buzz us in. Ain't this some shit I don't even have the code to enter my father's gates. I'm not really pressed about it, because I rarely come to see his crazy demented ass anyway. A few more unnecessary minutes flew by and he finally buzzed us in.

I swear this muthafucka lives to good. I scanned over the sprinklers that watered his perfect green grass the big as statue of himself took away from its elegance in my opinion. His house was huge. It was almost a replica of the White House.

"Wait here," I told Melinda. She frowned at me.

"I gotta pee."

"Hold it," I simply said to her then got out.

I shook my head as his goons searched me like I'm some nigga off the streets. That's my father, he don't trust nobody not even me. I can't say I blame him though. As I took the long walk to his office I tried to think back to the last time I saw him. It's no secret Pops and I don't see eye to eye about a lot things. I really can't stand the muthafucka but because he's my dad I try my best to respect him.

When I walk into the office his big burly ass is sitting behind his desk shirtless with a Cuban cigar dangling from his mouth. He reminded me a lot of the rapper Shug Knight just a much darker version.

"Sup Big Brian?" I said shaking his hand before taking a seat across from him.

"You tell me. I hope it's good since you coming through this time of morning. You know shit like this make's a nigga paranoid so I hope it's good," he said blowing smoke my way. I cleared my throat.

"I need your help."

"What's new?"

"It's my girl. She left me. I need you to find out where she at."

"Brian, Brian," he laughed shaking his head. "Still chasing pussy I see. The last one you got away with. But this one, I'm not so sure."

"Here we go!"

"I ain't about to make a long drawn out speech because I can look at your crazy ass and see you gone do what the fuck you want to do anyway. Just know this after everything you've worked for crumbles behind this bitch don't come asking me for nothing. No commissary money, conversation, Nothing! Just walk away Brian. I've never chased after a bitch and you shouldn't either. I taught you better than that. See you've got the game all fucked up. You wine and dine them. Treat em' like they worth something. In order to tame a bitch, you strip em'. Strip of their dignity, their respect, their self esteem. Make em' feel so low the only way the can climb back up is through you."

"She's different."

"You said the same shit about Macy," he smirked.

"She is."

"You've been warned. Don't ask me for shit Brian. When that cell door finally closes on your black ass just know at that moment you are dead to me."

"Here," I said handing him a piece of paper.

"What's this?"

"It's all her information; birthday, height, weight, and phone number. Everything about her is all there. "He nodded his head as he took the piece of paper out of my hand.

"I thought you would be different Brian. I thought you would keep our legacy going. I showed you a lot, let you experience a lot but you let that heart of yours get you in a lot of trouble. You should know me. One thing I can't stand is a soft ass nigga," he said banging his hand down on the desk.

That shit was loud. I almost jumped. I remained seated until he finished with his rampage. This is exactly why I hated my father. Instead of being supportive he always found a way to bring a nigga down.

A slight chill came over me as I walked out of his office and walked the long hall way that would eventually lead me to my exit. So many memories of this place I wanted to suppress and they slowly started to come to the surface. So many lives were taken here. I remember this one time Ace and I had spent the night. One of my father's goons had gotten out of pocket and talked back to him to hear him say it.

I think I was around thirteen or fourteen at the time. He called me to his office. Ace got to stay upstairs and watch television but he wanted to show me something. Told me this was a life lesson. I hated my father's *lessons*. "You gone learn how to run an empire," he said to me while unbuttoning his shirt and stepping out of his jeans. *"Once a mutha fucka steps out of line you strip him of everything. Right down to his man hood. Teach a nigga about talking back to me. Never bite the hand that feeds you,"* he snapped, pointing his thick ass finger in my face.

I stood there frozen as three men held the goon captive. At first I didn't understand why he was naked from the waist down. I can still hear him pleading.

"Come on B don't do this man. Please don't do this man. I'm sorry man. Ahhhh!"

I can still remember the look in his eyes as my father took away his man hood. I hated him even more after that day. I never wanted to be like him. I just wanted a family, someone to love me and take the pain away. I thought I found that in Savannah, guess I was wrong because she only made the pain worse.

Savannah

I was smiling from ear to ear. It felt good to laugh. Brandon had me cracking up as we talked about old times.

"Remember that time I took you to your doctor's appointment and we had to reschedule because you forgot your license," Brandon laughed. "That old ass receptionist went in on you, yo' that shit was hilarious."

"I don't remember."

"I bet you don't," he laughed. "She was like so if you were in a car accident no one would be able to identify you because you don't have any identification," he mocked. "That was funny. You didn't say much but the look on your face was priceless. Damn I wish I took your picture."

"Shut up," I said laughing. The receptionist did go in on me though. I try to respect my elders and she almost made me go there with her old ass. She had a point about the license but she kept going on and on about it. But because of her I try to make sure I have my license with me every where I go.

"I'm just saying that was a Kodak moment."

"Moving on." There was a brief pause.

"On a more serious note-,"

"Here we go," I said rolling my eyes towards the ceiling.

"I'm not about to ask twenty questions just the usual. Now if I didn't call to check on you, you probably be talking shit about me."

"No I wouldn't."

"You know females be tripping. Talking bout niggas ain't shit, the sex is whack just a whole bunch of unnecessary drama."

"Anyway, if you must know I'm doing ok. I'm thinking about going on a cruise, or just doing some traveling in general," I said. He sighed.

"So what about us?"

I cleared my throat because that threw me for a loop. He's the only person I've kept in contact with and just talking to him gives me life but as far as starting over, I haven't really put much thought into it. I kind of like the place we are in right now. To me a relationship would compromise that.

"Brandon-"

"Savannah."

"You know I'm with Brian," I lied.

"Yeah okay, if that's the case why you on the phone with me instead of him?" I sucked in some air. I haven't spoken to Brian since the night before he left for Miami. After a few odd moments of silence he apologized. "I'm sorry Savannah, I should have never asked. It's not the right time I know. It's hard."

"I know and I'm sorry but with everything going on in my life I can't even focus on a relationship right now. Let's just keep things the way they are and if something comes of it so be it."

"I really shouldn't be greedy since you didn't talk to me for a whole year. Then out of the blue you throw that come back pussy on me and now I'm feenin' like Jodeci."

"You are so corny," I laughed.

"You like it."

We conversed for another good forty-five minutes before I reluctantly ended the call. He informed me they never did find out who tried to break into my home. Just hearing that put a little fear in my heart and my thoughts immediately went to Brian. I sighed and prayed my suspicions aren't true. My life is so complicated and I wish I could close my eyes, and wish away all my fears, bring back the loved ones that I lost, and live happily ever after with Brandon. But in my world there is no such thing as a happy ending.

I'm feeling a sense of peace where I'm at right now. I know eventually I will have to go back to Maryland and tie up some loose ends but I officially plan on starting my life over in Georgia. I have more than enough money to do just that but I do want to rent out my old home. Since Zaheeda is down there that way maybe I can trust her to be an over seer of the property. So much I need to do but I just don't have the energy to do it. I place the phone back on the base and grabbed my cell phone that's been collecting dust since I got here. I connected it to the charger and waited a few minutes before powering it on.

As soon as I did it started singing. I knew my voicemail was probably full, and a few text messages started popping up. I checked my voicemail. I had two from Detective Harley. I frowned wondering what he wanted. Maybe he found a lead in the investigation. I searched through the night stand grabbed an envelope and a magic marker and quickly jotted his number down. I listened to the remaining messages even the ones from Roxie's bipolar ass. I should probably call her but I'm not in the mood to deal with her dramatics. I went through the remainder of my messages shot both Roxie and Zaheeda a text letting them know I was good and would be back on that side of town shortly and cut my phone off again before heading down stairs.

"Look who decided to join us," my Aunt Tammy sang as I walk into the kitchen. I smiled at my cousin Sabrina who was sitting at the table eating apple pie and ice cream. My eyes lit up. I know I've gained at least a good ten pounds eating up my Aunt's cooking. "Is that home made?"

"I'm insulted," Aunt Tammy said looking at me sideways.

"Sorry," I giggled as I quickly grabbed a bowl and spoon.

"So how's Brandon?" she asked.

"How do you know it was him?"

"Chile please," she said folding her arm across her chest. "So how is he?"

"He's doing alright," I said joining both her and my cousin at the table.

"You getting a little thick around the hips ain't you?" Sabrina joked.

"I'm trying to catch up to you. Why couldn't I take after you Aunt Tammy? I think you stole all that from mommy. I mean she was working with a little sumptin but not like you." Both her and my cousin Sabrina were thicker than a snicker.

"Girl hush," Aunt Tammy said waving me off. "Now back to you. What's going on with you and that man? Whatever happened to y'all? I thought you two were so Drunk in loveeeee," she sang swinging her head back and forth.

"What you know about Drunk in Love?" I laughed. She placed her hand on her wide hip.

"Humph, I'm old but I ain't cold," she said snapping her fingers in a circle three times. Me and Sabrina fell out laughing. She was right about that though. My Aunt still had it going on at the age of fifty five. Her caramel skin was flawless, not one blemish in sight. She had long curly eye lashes that brought out her beautiful bright brown eyes. She didn't look a day over forty. She's a fitness fanatic and got her thirty minutes of work out in at least five days out of the week.

"So back to you Ms. Thang, how are you holding up? I see you're smiling a lot more."

"I'm doing a lot better," I said shrugging my shoulders.

When I first arrived to Georgia I was a wreck. I know I stayed cooped up in the guest room for a week straight. Every night my Aunt Tammy would come in and pray over me. By the second week I really didn't have a choice but to get up. Aunt Tammy stood over my bed with a vase of cold water. "We can do this the hard way or the easy way," I remember her saying to me, so I chose the easy way.

"That's good. So how long do you plan on staying?"

"What! You trying to rid of me already?" I asked faking like my feelings were hurt.

"Girl, you should know me by now. If I wanted yo' ass out you'd be out." I laughed and shook my head.

"I don't know. I just need some time to regroup and get my thoughts together. I actually like it down here, think I might relocate."

"Oh really!"

"Yep."

"What about that man. What's his name Sabrina?"

"Huh?" Sabrina asked.

"You know Savannah's so called boyfriend."

"Oh Brian," Sabrina answered. "What about him?"

"Does he know you're down here?"

"No," I sighed.

"Why not?"

"I don't know. I just needed to get away and clear my head."

"So that included him too?"

I sighed not really in the mood to make Brian the topic of our discussion but I could tell by the way my Aunt was looking at me that she wasn't going to give this up. She's right though he's apart of what I needed to get away from.

"Yeah, I guess. I mean Brian's been great, but it just wasn't working for me."

"Why? Is it because of Brandon? " my Aunt asked raising an eyebrow.

"I don't know. It just wasn't it. I broke up with him but I don't think he gets it."

"What you mean you don't think he gets it?" Aunt Tammy asked snapping her neck back. "Does he need some help to understand that its over? You want me to break it down for him? You know I don't mind. I don't like him anyway," she said. I could tell by the look on her face she was dead serious. I shook my head no and laughed.

"I think he will get the memo now Aunt Tammy. Thanks anyway." I looked at Sabrina who simply shook her head. She knew her mom could get wild at times.

"Now, what happened between you and Brandon? It's obvious you still love that man since he knows you're down here and no one else does? Sabrina get me a glass of water, please."

"He cheated."

"I thought you guys worked past all that. Thank you baby," she said as Sabrina placed a glass of water in front of her.

"Well, we did but then . . . I . . . I," I paused. I hated to get into all this again because saying it out in the open sounds so stupid. It's still hard for me to believe that it happened my damn self. Both my aunt and cousin were looking at me waiting for me to finish, so I told them the story of how I walked in my home and found Brandon in bed with another woman.

"Whatttttttt!" Aunt Tammy said as she fanned herself and took a sip of her water. "Are you serious? You did right by leaving his trifling ass then. I know all hell broke loose after that. I know you beat that heifers ass and his too."

"Well, not exactly."

"What you mean not exactly."

"I just left." I looked from my aunt to my cousin and I knew that look all to well. I knew what they were thinking. Everybody says the same shit that I'm stupid for just turning around and leaving but that's what I did and I can't turn back the hands of time. I don't think I would change anything even if I could.

"You mean to tell me you just walked out of the house after you caught your man in bed with another woman. Girl I know your mama taught you better than that. I wish a nigga would bring a bitch up in my house where I pay the bills and lay my head at."

"Mom calm down," Sabrina frowned. "You act like it was you or something."

"I just can't believe you walked away. Well what did his sorry ass do?"

"Nothing. He was sleep, fully clothed except for his shirt and she was staring up at me butt ass naked."

"Girl you better than me cause I sho would have cut his little dangler right on off then beat her ass wit it afterwards."

"I know Aunt Tammy but that just ain't me."

"That's exactly why you got stuck in a relationship you don't want to be in."

"Well, there's a little more to the story. It's another reason why I left Maryland. This sounds crazy but I think someone purposely wanted to break up me and Brandon. I think someone is trying to ruin my life."

"That does sound crazy? Are you alright chile?" Aunt Tammy asked feeling my forehead. "Go get her some Tylenol or something she does feel a little warm," she said to Sabrina.

"Aunt Tammy, my life is complicated right now. Just hear me out." I told her about the conversation Brandon and I had regarding our little situation.

"Well damn, when you put it like that it does sound suspect," she frowned. "Brandon is smarter than that and like you said if he admitted the first time why wouldn't he admit to the second. It's probably ain't nobody but that crazy ass Roxie."

"Aunt Tammy I don' t think so," I said even though I was having thoughts about the possibility. She was never a big fan of Brandon. She always accused him of trying to tear of us apart.

"Well, you are welcomed to stay here as long as you like baby. I ain't know your life was a real life soap opera. I need a Valium. You want one?"

"I'm good," I laughed. I stood up. "Is it okay if I use your phone? Detective Harley called and left me a message. I'm trying to keep my cell phone off as much as possible."

"You don't even have to ask. You think they found something?"

"I don't know. I hope so. The suspense is gut wrenching. I hate the fact that the person who did this is still out there walking free while my parents are laid stiff in some damn coffin. Sorry Aunt Tammy."

"It's fine. Just know that God has a way of working things out."

"Amen to that."

Sabrina

"That poor child," my mother said as she got up and grabbed the dishes that we left behind.

I held back the tears that lingered in the corners of my eyes. I feel so bad for Savannah. I can only imagine what she's feeling right now. I mean I lost my father a few years ago, to cancer but we knew it was coming. Just the thought of someone harming your parents has to fuck with a person heavy. Hell it was fucking with me. We moved along time ago because we found a treatment center for my father and we figured he would get better care here and he did, but that took us away from Savannah, Aunt Karen and Uncle Gerald.

I even stayed with them one summer when my father got real bad and my mother was on the verge of a nervous breakdown. Spending time with them took me away from the personal hell I was experiencing at home. Roxie was something else even back then. She didn't like when I was around. She wanted Savannah all to herself, but as always Savannah is to blind and naïve to see it. I even noticed the animosity she held towards Gabby.

Just thinking about Gabby made my stomach hurt. This secret that I've been carrying around hurts to the depths of my soul. The guilt consumes me to the point I get sick. I know she killed Gabby. You know what they say the quiet ones are sneaky and that's me down to a T. My hot ass was out with Sterling, Brandon's brother. He was the shooting guard for the boys Varsity basketball team. We didn't do anything that night just let him suck on my tities and play in the kitty. I was scared to go all the way he was working with a monster.

I'm two years older than Savannah so I believe I was fourteen at the time, just a freshman in high school but I looked older than my age because of the serious curves my mama blessed me with. He'd just dropped me off a couple houses down. I'd just made it home when I looked across the street and noticed Gabby and Roxie walking hand in hand. The neighborhood was still pret-

ty much asleep, it was still dark outside but the lighting from the porch lights helped me identify them as they giggled without a care in the world. I didn't think much of it at the time, as I sit back and look on it I wish I did.

The next morning when I found out what happened to Gabby I was sick with so much guilt I couldn't bring myself to face Savannah or my Aunt and Uncle for a whole week. I just couldn't do it. I remember asking my mother if Roxie was okay too and she just gave me this strange look.

"Of course she is, why wouldn't she be?" I remember she asked me.

I don't remember what I told her but after that I stayed away as much as possible. I knew Roxie killed Gabby I just had this feeling. It was me who made an anonymous phone call to Detective Harley and told him that I saw Roxie and Gabby walking down the street earlier that morning but nothing came of it. So I just held onto my secret and the guilt that came with it. A good thirteen years later and the guilt is still weighing me down.

"Sabrina what's wrong?" my mother asked me startling out of my thoughts.

"Nothing," I half smiled.

"Then what are all these tears for?" she asked handing me some tissues. She gently rubbed my back. "You want to talk about it?"

She had no idea just how badly I did. It was on the tip of my tongue as I stared at the concern in her eyes. But even now I couldn't bring myself to say what was really on my mind. So I simply shook my head no.

"What's done in the dark Sabrina will eventually come to the light. You're too old to be holding onto to secrets. The sooner you get it out the better off you will be." She kissed me on my forehead and left me in the kitchen. I sighed because I knew she was right.

Roxie

"Please, don't stop," I begged as I bit my bottom lip and rotated my hips. As usual Andre was putting in work, with his face in between my thighs sucking on this pussy like he missed it. "Got damn," I yelled as he placed two fingers inside of my wetness stroking my inner walls with such perfection it felt like he was creating art. I arched my back and grabbed the head board as I prepared to release but he stopped. My eyes flew open, my pussy still throbbing in anticipation.

"Shit," he said jumping off the bed. He grabbed his clothes and stumbled around the room trying to put them on.

"What the fuck is wrong with you?" I snapped. I needed him to finish what he started. Besides he asked me to come over. Talking bout he missed me. We hadn't kicked it in a while and I had some time to kill before I was supposed to meet up with Damon so I figured why not.

"Dre, baby where you at?"

"So I guess we won't be finishing shit," I said rolling my eyes into the back of my head. I was pissed. I rolled off the bed and found the dress I wore earlier and quickly slipped it on. By now I could hear her foot steps. That was his wife. She was supposed to be going out of town, she must have doubled back on his ass. The nerve of this bitch.

"Fuck! Fuck! Roxie you gotta hide. Get in the closet he whispered as he stood by the bedroom door. "Or the bathroom I really don't care, just hurry up and do it," he snapped.

I almost laughed at his ass. He had to be out of his damn mind if he thought I was about to hide up in somebody's damn closet. I'm too old for that shit. He should have had everything figured out before he invited me over. Hide! Tuh!

"What!" I said looking at his ass like he was crazy.

"Shhhh," he said placing a finger to his lips while he jumped around like he had to pee. "Roxie please," he begged.

"Dre." His wife was right outside of the door.

"You better go see about your wife. I'm too old to be hiding in somebody's closet," I shrugged. He gave me this crazy sideways look. I think he wanted to hit me. I wish that nigga would. I got a fresh blade in my pocket book that hasn't been broken in yet.

"Dre, who the fuck is that? I know you don't have some bitch up in my got damn house. You better open this muthafuckin door," she yelled as she literally tried to break the door down.

I slipped my feet in my boots, grabbed my purse and made sure my blade and mace were handy. Dre stood there while his wife continued to bang and scream on the other side of the door. I had to do a double take. He had tears in his eyes. See this the shit I be talking about. Men so quick to fuck the next bitch but as soon as they get caught they crying and being extra. Learn how to control yourself and keep ya dick in ya pants if you can't handle the consequences is all I'm saying.

"Are you going to open the door or what?" I asked giving my nails a quick once over. It's time for a fill in, might do that tomorrow. "Oh you know what I think I left one of my bags in your car. Yeah matter of fact I did. That Tiffany bracelet you bought me I left it in your console."

I swear if looks could kill I'd be six feet under. But I was dead serious. He took me on a mini shopping spree before we ended up in his bed. I wanted everything that was owed to me including that bracelet. He had the nerve to roll his eyes before unlocking the door. He tried to ease it open but his wife wasn't having it. She pushed the door open damn near causing Andre to fly into the wall.

Whoa! I wasn't expecting Precious but here she is in the flesh. Got damn this bitch is big. Then she had the nerve to have on leggings. I looked from her to Andre and I would have never pictured the two together. I use to fuck around with him back when he was a bachelor. He wasn't looking for anything serious and I wasn't either. He's into real estate so when the market kind of went left his pockets went south and so did I. We kept in contact here and there recently he hit me up saying he wanted to link up. He told me he was married but that didn't make my business bad.

Maybe it's just me but they look like an odd couple. He's average height about five ten, five eleven, skin the color of dark chocolate, those chinky eyes and high cheek bones. His head was bald and smoother than a baby's ass. This chick here, I mean I'll giver her props she's pretty but she just doesn't seem like his type. She looks back and forth between Dre and I. Were fully dressed but she's no dummy. I could see it in her eyes she was about to attack. She slapped the shit out of Andre. That muthafucka went flying backwards. I would have laughed but I knew I was next. I grabbed my mace and doused her big ass before she could get a good one in on me.

"Bitch," she snarled at me as she covered her eyes. I pushed her with all my might and she bounced off the bed before landing hard on the floor.

"Roxie." I whipped around and mace Andre's ass too. I shoved him just as hard and he ended up back in the floor beside his wife.

I grabbed his wallet, his car keys and ran. I took bills out of his wallet and threw it on the ground. I hit the unlock button on his Benz. The sound caused me to jump a little but it didn't deter me from my mission. I looked back at his house, the coast was still clear. I opened the door, searched through his console until I found my bracelet. I smiled like a kid in the candy store. I jogged the few blocks to my cars. It was cold as a muthafucka but hey at least I got my bracelet.

*****

"Ace," he moaned as he arched his back and fell face first onto the bed.

I frowned wondering if he was referring to the same Ace I know. Humph let me find out. The smell that bounced around in the air made my stomach churn. I carefully hopped off the bed and carried the dildo to the bathroom and dropped it in the trash can. I grabbed the air freshener and sprayed. Afterwards I washed my hands and joined Damon in the bed.

"Soooooooooooo, who's Ace?" I asked being nosey.

He lay flat on his stomach, looked at me and smiled. It's a shame he's playing for the home team because this man is beautiful. He looks like he's from an island. His hair was like silk, his bright honey colored eyes bought out his smooth olive skin. This man was fine. His body was sculpted and toned to perfection. I could only lick my lips and simply wonder what the Mandigo between his legs could do. Despite his age he was in perfect shape. He acts younger than he is anyway.

"A nigga I work for."

"Hmmmm, another down low brother like you?"

"Hell no," he laughed. "He has no idea. If he knew I looked at him in that way I'd be laid up in somebody's casket."

"Oh. So the dude you talking about his last name wouldn't happen to be Davis would it?" He didn't say anything but the look on his face confirmed my assumptions. "So you work for him?"

"Yeah, I handle the business aspect of his club. Make sure contracts are legit and shit like that. I also handle his power of attorney yada yada."

"Oh, I see," I said nodding my head. "So you know Brian too." He sucked his teeth and rolled his eyes. "What was that about?" I laughed. He looked at me long and hard like he wanted to say something. I didn't press the issue but held my breath because I had a feeling what he has to say is going to be juicy.

"Let's just say Brian and I engage in activities other than business."

"What?" I shot up. "Hold up, Brian taking it up the ass?"

"No," he said shaking his head. "To let him tell it giving or receiving anal is gay and he swears ain't nothing gay about receiving head from a man."

"You lying," I said looking at him sideways.

"Sips tea," he said sipping from an imaginary cup with his pinky finger in the air.

Damn shit just keeps coming out about this dude. I wonder what the hell I'm going to find out next. I tried to warn Vee's stupid ass but nope. She swears I'm just man bashing. I can't wait until all this shit comes to light so I can tell her ass I told you so.

"His ego is the size of Texas but his equipment is a third of Maryland. That nigga is working with a baby," he laughed holding up his pinky finger. I couldn't even control my laughter. "He be talking shit too talking bout can I handle that big dick. Girl I have to strain to see that muthafucka little as it is and he be calling it King Kong. He is putting that name to shame."

"You ain't right," I said shaking my head laughing.

"But they say the apple doesn't fall to far from the tree," he said shrugging his shoulders. I damn near snapped my neck as I looked over at him.

"What is that supposed to mean?"

"Just what it means?"

"Big Brian!" I questioned with a raised eyebrow. I never would have pegged that cold muthafucka as a shit pusher but you never know who's undercover now and days.

"Humph, I'm just gone sip the hell out of this tea," he responded giving me that knowing glance. "You'd be surprised how many dudes out here living a double life."

"By all means do tell."

Roxie

I climbed off my treadmill and bent over taking a breather. I love working out it helps me think. "Whew," I breathed in deep and headed straight to the shower. I stripped down to my birthday suit and turned on the shower. When it was desired temperature I hopped right on in. The hot water helped work out the tension in my muscles. I washed my hair and stayed in there a good thirty minutes before stepping out.

I grabbed a towel walked back into my bedroom, lotioned my body and put on a pair of leggings and a tank top. I grabbed my phone and checked my missed calls and texts. A message or phone call from Vee would have made my day. She did text me one day out of the blue to let me know that she was okay. I tried to call her back but it went straight to voice mail. As much I wanted her to come home I needed her to stay where ever she is a little longer just until I got shit in motion. Hopefully everything I got planned will happen before the holidays. I hope she decides to come back home by then.

I'm waiting on Prince to make his move. We haven't spoken since that little incident I had with Bri. She swore me up and down that she hasn't kept in contact with him either. Apparently that muthafucka was making time for her because she told me he's been blowing her up nonstop, and one night he even came to her house but she wouldn't answer the door. I'm not gone front hearing that had me in my feelings.

Since Mr. Prince wants to play hard to get I decided to get his attention another way. I've been popping up at his parent's house here and there, conveniently when his mother isn't home. I think his father Harold has a little crush on me. When he rubs my back I can tell the touch is a little more than just friendly. It's all good because I plan on capitalizing on that very soon. Matter of fact think I'm going to make another appearance over there tomorrow and see if I can cause a little friction between us. I need to improvise just in case Damon has no plans of considering the proposition I offered him. My phone begins to ring rocking me out of my thoughts. I rolled my eyes at the name that flashes across my phone.

"Yes."

"Roxie, do you know my wife ended up in the hospital behind that shit you did? She has fucking asthma," Andre snapped over the phone.

"It was self defense. If I didn't defend myself I probably would be in the damn hospital. You didn't tell me your wife was a fucking line backer, shit!" I was no match for her, so I have to do whatever means necessary to save this pretty ass.

"She wanted to press charges."

"Good luck on that one," I snapped.

"Why you have to steal my got damn wallet?"

"I didn't," I lied.

"Whatever!"

"Well, all this could have been avoided if you'd just planned things a little more carefully. I don't do closet's or bathrooms boo." There was a brief silence.

"So . . . uh . . . when we gone finish what we started?" he asked.

I had to take the phone away from my ear and look at it. Typical ain't shit muthafucka. I shake my head because his wife probably made it too easy for his ass. He probably apologized, bought some flowers, a little bit of jewelry and all is well in her eyes. Her self esteem probably allows her to stay with a man that ain't no good. Ladies we've got to do better. Don't make it easy for his ass or he sure will go out there and do it again. I placed the phone back to my ear.

"I ain't coming to your house," I finally answered sucking my teeth.

"I was thinking the Hyatt."

"Make sure you leave your wife at home."

"You got jokes."

"I'm dead ass serious. Just give me a time and place I'm there. Just make sure you have some dividends waiting on a bitch."

"Anything for you boo," he said. I rolled my eyes and laughed.

"Whatever, call me later."

"Bye!"

After my phone call I decided to send Harold a text.

Me: I hate to bother you but have you talked to Prince? He still hasn't called me or anything.

I doodled around for a good forty five minutes. I did my hair did another bout of sit ups and watched some tv before he text me back.

Harold: No baby I haven't.

Baby, I thought.

Me: I hate to keep bothering you with this but I don't know what I did. I love your son very much and I just wish we could sit down and talk things out. He could at least tell me what I did.

Harold: Your right baby girl. I don't know what's wrong with that boy. His mother and I didn't raise him like this.

Me: I just want to know what I did wrong?

Harold: I'll talk to him.

Me: Thank you

Yesssss! This is what I plan on doing until I finally get a response from his ass. I know he had to be tired of his father contacting him on my behalf I shouldn't have to hunt his raggedy ass down anyway. I upgraded his ass.

Just like I suspected Prince contacted me a week later. I didn't think he would wait that damn long, but he called so it's all good.

"What's up Roxie?" he asked like he was annoyed. I frowned. This nigga is really feeling himself. He better be lucky I let him anywhere near this royal pussy. I sucked my teeth and breathed in deep.

"I should ask you. What's been up with you lately?"

"Just got a lot of shit on my mind."

"We need to talk."

"I can agree on that." There was brief pause.

"Sooooooo-,"

"I'll be by there sometime tonight," he said shortly.

"Aight," I sighed. "That's cool." I waited for a response but never received one. I took the phone away from my ear only to realize that muthafucka had the nerve to hang up on me. I sucked my teeth and set my phone down, because I've accomplished part of my mission. Now all I need is to get his fingerprints and I'm good.

Prince

I ain't even in the mood to deal with Roxie or her drama. That bitch was last week and I really shouldn't have to explain shit to her. My distance and lack of interest should be self explanatory but I guess just like the average bitch she needs closure. I don't know why my father calling me on her behalf anyway. Roxie and I haven't been kicking it that long so it's not like they've established a relationship. Matter of fact I'm feeling some kind of way about it.

I snorted a line, and rubbed my nose. My habit has gotten out of hand. I use to fuck with it here and there when I was younger but now I can't go a day without that white girl tickling my nose. I allowed the drug to race through my blood stream, then grabbed my keys and headed out the door.

My music was on full blast and I swung my head from side to side to keep in sync with the beat. Bri came to my mind and I missed her like crazy. It's fucked up how we became as one but the heart wants what the heart wants and all I want is her. Just thinking about the treasure she got between her legs had my dick hard. She caught my eye when I went to Savannah's parent's funeral with Roxie. I always thought Roxie was bad but she ain't got shit on Bri. Maybe the eyes but other than that it's all Bri.

She's been acting funny lately. I haven't seen her ass in a minute and I feel like I'm dying inside. She won't answer my calls, my text, nothing. I even stopped by her house. I knew she was inside because I seen her peek out the window but she didn't even answer the damn door. I guess it's true what they say about karma, she's a real bitch because the same shit I was doing to Roxie, Bri is doing to me.

"Cause I'm in love wit a stripper. She poppin' she rollin', she rollin'. She climbin' that pole and I'm in love wit a stripper. She trippin', she playin', she playin'. I'm not goin' nowhere girl I'm stayin'. I'm in love with a stripper," I sang along with T pain's *I'm in love with a stripper.*

Roxie must have been waiting for me because I didn't even get a chance to knock. She opened the door and glared at me with her hand on her hip. I wasn't fazed by her attitude. I guess she could tell because she smiled and pulled me in for a hug.

"I miss you," she sighed into my chest. My arms remained at my side.

"Roxie."

"Just playing," she said backing away from me. "Come on in," she said stepping aside and allowing me to enter. "Come on I'm making fruit salad," she said walking back towards the kitchen like shit between us is kosher.

I couldn't stop myself from looking at her fat ass if I wanted to. She had damn near everything her mama gave her hanging out the tiny ass shorts she had on. My man hood jumped in appreciation. I shook my head and tried to stay focus on what I came here to do . . . but I still might bless her with some break up dick.

"Here," she said handing me a butcher knife.

"What you giving me this for?" I frowned.

"I need you to cut the water melon for me. Please," she pouted poking her lip out.

"Aight ma, now put that lip back in," I said taking the knife out of her hand. She grabbed the water melon and placed it on the counter. She hopped on a bar stool and started slicing up strawberries. This felt weird. "You wanted to talk," I said before stabbing the watermelon. She sighs.

"I'll be right back."

"Okay," I said watching her walk away. It took her a little longer than I expected so I got comfortable. I sat down ate slice of water melon and damn near ate all the strawberries she cut up. When she walked back into the kitchen she dropped a bag at my feet. I popped a strawberry in my mouth and looked at it. "What's that?"

"You know all the shit you left over here, a couple of shirts, a few boxers, a pair of shoes and a watch."

"Good looking out," I said looking at her sideways. She's actually taking this better than I expected. I'm just bracing myself for the questions and whether or not I should tell her the truth. She sat down on the stool and looked at the empty bowl of strawberries in front of her and frowned. "I'm sorry ma," I laughed as she looked up at me.

Is this how a break up is supposed to be? I'm waiting on the fist to fly, ready to be called every name in the book followed by you ain't shit but from the looks of things I don't think that's happening. She carefully grabbed the knife I used and placed it on top of the refrigerator. I thought that was odd but it's her shit. She hopped up on the stool and placed her elbows on the counter.

"You know Prince, we had fun. I had a feeling it wouldn't last long but like I said it was fun while it lasted," she said shrugging her shoulders.

"I'm sorry things didn't work out between us."

"No biggie," she said shrugging her shoulders grabbing some more strawberries.

Damn, I'd be lying if I said my ego wasn't bruised. She was singing a different tune before now she's sitting here as cold as ice like this break up doesn't mean shit. If I didn't know any better I'd think her ass is bipolar.

"So, this is it huh?"

"Yep, I guess it is," she said nodding her head. An awkward silence stood between us before she started talking again. The look she had on her face made my heart skip a couple of beats. "You know when you play with fire you get burned Prince."

"I know," I laughed trying to keep the mood light.

"Sooooooooo, how's Bri?"

"Who?"

"Nigga you heard me," she said smacking her lips. "Ain't no need in lying about it because I already know." She sucked her teeth and rolled her eyes. She sat back and folded her arms across her chest waiting for me to respond. She had a point; I really had no reason to lie. Even though in the back of my mind I wonder how she knows and if she is the reason Bri has done a disappearing act on me.

"Roxie, I know it's fucked up. I never meant to hurt you-," She doubled over in laughter. She was laughing so hard she had tears in her eyes. I frowned wondering what the fuck is so damn funny. I'm trying to be sentimental and sensitive towards her feelings and she up here laughing at me like I'm a damn joke or something.

"Nigga please. You've served your purpose," she said wiping the tears from her.

"Fuck you then," I said bending over and grabbing my bag of clothes. "I still wish you the best."

"Same here. Good luck in trying to turn that hoe into a wife."

"The same could be said about you right?" I snapped. I turned around ready to leave. My anger was about to get the best of me and I didn't want to snap on her bipolar ass. I was hoping she would stay her wishy washy ass in the kitchen but nope, she followed me.

"I've known Bri a long time," she sighed. "You don't have what it takes to make a bitch like her settle down. The money is good, just enough to make her stay but err a, other than that I don't see it happening boo."

I shook my head because in my mind she is just another black woman scorned. But I'll give her that. She has every right to be mad so I ain't even gone sweat the slick talk. I open the front door and walked out without even acknowledging her. I tried to apologize but it's no use. She's seeing red right now and I figure better for me to get out of dodge. You never know what a bitch might stoop to when she gets angry and I ain't trying to end up in jail or a hospital tonight.

"She's fucking Ace," she yelled at me. I turned around and she's standing there with this smirk on her face.

"Yeah okay Roxie," I said opening my car door. Bitches get grimey when they desperate.

"You can't tell me she hasn't been acting a little different. I know she has that's because she's found a bigger and stronger dick to hold in her mouth."

She hit a sore spot when she said that because Bri has been showing her ass. She hasn't answered any of my text, phone calls, emails nothing. I wasn't about to give Roxie the satisfaction of knowing she was right. I know my face probably betrayed me and turned a shade darker. If she is fucking with that nigga Ace over me I ain't gone lie that shit fucks with me a little bit. Bri knows I can't stand that muthafucka.

"Bye Roxie." I didn't even realize she'd come down off her porch until I was inside my car and happened to look up and she was standing right outside my car. She smirked as she walked around to the driver's side.

"Just a fair warning. You might want to live everyday like it's your last."

"What the fuck is that supposed to mean?" I snapped. I know this bitch ain't threatening me.

"You gone regret the day you *ever* fucked over a bitch like me."

We stared at each other for I don't know how long. You know this bitch didn't even blink. She had me shook a little bit I can't even front. She fucked with me mentally and stripped me of my man hood. I hate when I allow a bitch to get the best of me. Chills rolled off my spine as I thought about what she just said to me; because I had a feeling she was going to make good on that promise. She smiled at me as she slowly back peddled towards her house. I didn't move until she finally made her way into the house. I could feel my heart racing in my chest.

"Damn, I done fucked up."

*****

"Bri!" I yelled as I stood on her front step banging on her front door.

I know she's home because her car is outside, plus she must have forgotten to turn her cell phone off. It started singing when I called it and then her dumb ass tried to cut it off in mid ring. Dead give away. The hawk is out, my hands are shaking from the cold but I ignored it. Love will make you do the craziest shit.

Maybe I am a sucker for love. Maybe Ace and Brian are right about me. I do it every time. Fall for a big butt and a smile and in the end I get burned. I stood back and re-evaluated myself. I like to think of myself as a boss. I got money, my own crib, a nice whip, I shouldn't have to beg to keep a woman's attention but that's exactly what I'm doing. I circled around the house ignoring my gut telling me it's time to leave.

My pride was buried six feet deep because ten minutes later I'm still begging and pleading on her front door. I looked like a damn fool but I couldn't help it. I love this girl. I'm willing to give up everything for her ass if she'd just let me. We can run away together. I need to get the fuck away anyway. This shit between Brian and Roxie is about to hit the damn fan and I ain't trying to get shitted on. I should have told Brian about Roxie's ass the minute she started talking crazy but I didn't. If I told him now I know his crazy ass will look at me funny and there's no telling what he might do. My phone started vibrating in my pocket. I grabbed it. As soon as I read her text message my heart sank.

Bri: *It's over Prince.*
Me: *What!*
Bri: *It's not working.*
Me: *Open the mutha fuckin' door.*
Bri: *Go home Prince.*

I can't believe this shit. I stared at my phone before looking back at the door expecting her to at least show me some respect and come down and face me like a woman but it never happened. I thought about Roxie. Damn it didn't take Karma long to live up to her legacy. I knew Bri had a reputation but I was willing to look past all that. I wanted to wife that girl and throw dirt on that old saying you can't turn a hoe into a house wife. Guess the joke is on me. I dialed her number. I needed answers and I wasn't in the mood to have a conversation through text messages, but she sent me straight to voice mail.

I ran my hand over my face, and let out a frustrated sigh. I looked around the neighborhood. It was a nice middle class set up. She wasn't doing bad for herself, but I was helping her out with that. I just paid her rent and the car note on the new Lexus she just got. She played me and that shit is slowly chopping at my pride and ego. I called her ass again and she directed me to voicemail. It's over between us and there ain't shit I can do about it. I'm too old to be standing out here begging for a bitch anyway. Damn. But before I leave I need to know one thing.

Me: *Is it true?*

Bri: Huh?????

Me: You fucking with Ace now?

Bri: I didn't think she was gone tell you. I didn't mean for you to find out this way but yes me and Ace have been kicking it for a while. He was before you, I swear.

Me: Miss me with that bull shit. It's cool. Make sure you tell that nigga don't let me catch him sleepin'. Dueces.

"I can't believe I wasted my time on another bum bitch."

Brandon

"So what's the plan? You trying to make Georgia your new home or what?"

"I don't know. I might. It's nice down here."

Hearing her say that crushed me. I know deep down in my heart Savannah and I could never be together but I would love for us to be friends if that's even possible. I'm still trying to find out how the hell I ended up in bed with another woman. To hear Savannah tell it I was passed out while some naked woman was lying in bed with me. I've racked my brain hard and I don't know what the hell she's talking about. I will never say it to Savannah but I wonder if she is making the whole thing up. If she is she convinced the hell out of me.

"What you think ole boy gone say about that? You plan on letting him move down there with you?"

"Here we go," she said sucking her teeth. I laughed because I knew her eyes were probably rolling in the back of her head by now. "Why do you always bring him up whenever we talk?"

Did she really even have to ask?

"Real talk, you know I'm jealous. You were mines first and any man that comes after me I'm going to have a problem with."

"Awe," she cooed.

"I'm serious."

"Oh really?"

"Really!"

"So what about that chick?"

"What chick?" I frowned.

"Don't play dumb. You was chilling wit her at the club, I bumped into you and her at Starbucks, then y'all was out and about shopping. You remember what chick I'm talking about now."

"You jealous?" I chuckled.

"Nope."

"Why you lying?"

"I'm not and don't try to change the subject. Who is she?"

"Just a friend. Why you care?"

"I don't care, I'm just being nosey."

"Yeah okay," I said sucking my teeth. There was a pause before she asked again.

"So who is she?"

"She's just a friend. I just told you that."

"Hmmm, a friend huh? So ya'll fucking or what?"

I had to pull the phone away from my ear. Savannah usually doesn't ask questions so I know she's jealous. As badly as I wanted to lie I knew that I couldn't. Even though my answer might break her heart she deserved to know the truth.

"Once," I replied. I heard her exhale.

"So it's nothing serious?"

"For you not to care you sure are asking a lot of questions. Let me find out you still got feelings for ya boy," I laughed.

"I will always have feelings for you Brandon. You can't get over someone just like that. We were together for years. I thought you were my forever and a day but not every fairy tale has a happy ending."

I heard her sniffle and I knew she was crying. I hated that I was the source of those tears. Damn I wish I could hold her and take away any doubt or fear that she may have in her heart. She's the only woman that has ever pulled that mushy side out of me. She has my heart and I don't know how to get it back. I doubt I ever will.

"I never meant to hurt you Savannah," I whispered. It was on the tip of my tongue. I wanted to get it off my chest but then again I didn't. I knew if I told her the full story about my infidelity that would be the end of us. She deserved to know, but this is something that needed to be said in person. No matter the consequences.

"Moving on," Savannah said after we shared an awkward silence.

"When are you coming back to Maryland?"

"I don't know," she yawned. "Don't keep asking me. With the way things are going I really ain't trying to come back. I might just look into selling my house, even if it means taking a loss. I just want to start over. I need a fresh start. I'm tired of caring about every body else. It's time I start thinking about me."

"Amen to that."

"Whatever," she said.

"I'm serious. You know I want what's best for you."

"Same here."

"So . . . what color panties you got on?"

"Doo doo brown," she said smacking her lips.

"Oh word. I bet that shit sexy as fuck. Send me a pic."

"I ain't sending you nothing. That's so high school."

"I remember you use to send me pictures all the time. Matter of fact I think I still got some on my phone."

"Really?"

"Yep."

"I'm getting ready to go. I'll holler at you later. Are my where abouts still safe. Has anybody been asking about me?"

"No your secret is still safe with me. Just wish I could spend the holidays with you?" I held my breath not really expecting her to agree but after a brief silence, she did.

"Okay."

*****

I can't believe she said yes. I'm running around my office like a chicken with its head cut off. I was tempted to call her back and make sure she wasn't playing, but I knew it had to be official since she sent me her Aunts address. Boss man was nice and allowed me to take the entire week after Thanksgiving off. He knows I work hard and rarely take days off so he didn't have a problem with it.

After booking my flight and tying some loose ends up at the office I decided to head home and pack. So imagine my surprise when I walk outside and Brandi's Jeep is parked right next to me. That took me by surprise because we haven't spoken in a minute. It was fucked how I did her though. I mean I thought Brandi and I always had an understanding that we were just friends, but I knew she wanted something more but I couldn't give her that. I needed a friend and she was that for me. But one night things took a left turn and we ended up in bed together. Just my luck Savannah called the same night.

Some may call me every dog in the damn book but I will drop everything when it comes to Savannah. I never intended to hurt anybody or throw shade but I took the call. Brandi was there so I went to the bathroom for some privacy. When I returned she was gone. I've sent a few texts and let her know I was sorry but I think she is still in her feelings about the situation. I can't blame her and I never pressed the issue but to see her here now, is weird. She put her window down as I walked up to her.

"What's up?" I asked not hiding that I was surprised to see her. I hope whatever she had to say she said it quick because it's cold as a bitch outside. I tried to wrap my North Face tighter around my body.

"We,"

"So, is this the bitch you been dodging me for?"

"Fuck!" I mumbled under my breath as I looked towards the sky. You think she would get the hint. I haven't touched her in months and she still carrying on like were in a relationship. I need to file sexual harassment on her ass and be done with it. We fucked a couple times that's it. I never gave her the impression that it was more than just sex between us but it ain't registering. I shouldn't have mixed business with pleasure. I wished she would have stayed in Miami permanently.

"Don't get quiet now nigga. Speak," Melinda snapped.

"Are you serious right now?" I asked looking at her sideways. I swear this bitch ain't worth the headache. Her pussy wasn't even all that. Now her head game I give her mad props for but still it ain't even worth the headache of dealing with her crazy ass.

"Naw I'm just standing out here in thirty degree weather for my health," she said placing her hand on her hip. "You know what Brandon I always thought you were a nice guy. What did I do to deserve this? You said you loved me."

"Melinda, I'm gone need you to find your Xanax, Zoloft, Ambien or whatever the hell it is you taking and get the hell on wit that bullshit. You're fucking delusional. I mean fucking crazy. You know good and got damn well I never told you no shit like that."

Standing here going back with that loophole had me aggravated. Brandi surprisingly sat back quietly as we went back and forth. I think she found the situation amusing because she had this smirk on her face. After a heated argument I threatened Melinda with sexual harassment and she stomped her delusional ass to her car all the while flipping me the bird, making a scene and complete ass of her self. I hope all this shit was on tape because I know I have to do something about this crazy chick. She's off her rocker and there's no telling what she might do. I've avoided her for long enough something had to give.

"Another one of your conquest," Brandi smirked.

"No," I frowned. "It wasn't even like that between me and her. She knows that."

"Obviously not."

"I don't even want to talk about it anymore. So what brings you by here."

"Well, I've been trying to catch you at home but you're always MIA so the next best place is here."

"Okay what's good?"

"We need to talk."

"About?" I asked checking the time on my watch. I hate to brush her off but I got shit to do so I decided to jump the gun and give her formally what she was looking for and what she is properly owed, an apology. "Let me start off by giving you a formal apology. You know I'm not a bad guy. I don't set out to intentionally hurt people. I'm sorry about how things went down between us. It was wrong for me to leave you like that, but . . . at the same time I told you from the jump I just wanted to be friends. I wasn't looking for anything serious."

"Well, I think it's a little too late for that."

"What is that supposed to mean?" I asked confused.

"I'm pregnant."

As soon as the words left her mouth it seemed like time stopped. I replayed her words over and over in my mind. I stood there waiting for her to crack a smile but she didn't. She can't be serious.

"By who?" I asked. She snapped her neck back and rolled her eyes like she was insulted, but I don't give a damn. A baby is serious business. We only fucked once and I used protection. "You muthafucka," she said holding up a pregnancy test. I looked at it and gave her the screw face. "Man get the fuck outta here with that bullshit," I said waving her off. I'm not one to skip out on my responsibilities but she was trying to sale me on the ole okie doke. I never thought Brandi was that type but these thirsty bitches have no shame. When you dry you'll do just about anything to get a damn drink. "I'll holler at you Brandi," I said grabbing my keys. I hit the button to unlock it.

"Oh, I see you trying to play a bitch. It's all good just make sure you run me my check muthafucka."

"Yeah okay," I laughed as I threw up a pair of deuces. I dipped inside of my car and watched as Brandi flipped me the bird before pulling off. I glanced down at my crotch and shook my head. "This is all your fault." I really do need to learn how to keep my dick in my pants. Too many crazy bitches getting attached to it.

Brian

This nigga is playing with my emotions. Big Brian has connections and it shouldn't take him this long to find out what the fuck I need. He's playing games. That's my father though. He always has to be in control. Thanksgiving is just days away and still no word from Savannah. This shit is eating me up inside. Each day that passes without knowing where she is destroys pieces of my soul. Damn I hate that I love that girl so much. If I could walk away I would, but I can't. I try to keep myself from thinking about her but I can't.

That girl has my heart and there's nothing I can do about it. Well I might have to kill her ass if she's been keeping time with some random nigga. I don't think Savannah's like that though. She's a good girl. I just wish she would've confided in me about what the hell she is going through. I think it might have something to do with her parents. Yeah that's what it is, but she could have talked to me about that. She didn't have to run away. Who does that?

This sitting and waiting has me paranoid. I can't take the suspense or pressure any more. I have to know where she is. Everything has gone to shit since she's been gone. I can't eat, I can't sleep, I can't do anything. Ace has been handling everything at the club and Miami has been put on hold. I thought it was best. I hated to put everything on him but with me being in this condition, I ain't no good to anybody.

"You good baby?" Melinda asked before massaging my shoulders.

"Yeah," I mumbled grabbing the glass filled with Jack Daniel sitting on the table and throwing it back. "Can I get another?" I said dangling the empty glass in front of her face. She snatched it out my hand and rolled her eyes. "Tough day at work?"

"Like you care. All you worried about is your precious Savannah. What is so special about that goofy looking bitch anyway?"

"Hey watch ya mouth."

"That's exactly what the fuck I mean. This bitch up and left your stupid ass high and dry and you telling me to watch my mouth. She got you up here looking all kinds of dumb but you still chasing after her ass."

"I don't recall asking for your opinion. So shut the fuck up and fix me my got damn drink."

"Fuck you," she snapped and hurled the empty glass at me. It missed me by a couple of inches. I jumped to my feet but before the glass even hit the wall she was gone. Just like a bitch to hit and run.

I wasn't about to sit here and entertain her bipolar ass either. I had more important shit to deal with. My father is tripping and he ain't been answering his phone. I hate popping up over his place unannounced because you never know what kind of mood that crazy muthafucka in but I need answers. I don't ask him for much. The only time I come to him is when I really need something and I really need to know where Savannah is.

At this point in our relationship I don't know if it's even worth saving. I just need to know where the fuck she at so I can put her out of her misery. This shit has gone on long enough. I tried to love her. I've tried to be patient but she keeps testing my hand. And a man like me can only take so much until I'm pushed over the edge. She's sealed her fate. I wined and dined that girl, and showed her nothing but the upmost respect. She has me up here looking a damn fool chasing behind her.

The reality of what this shit is hurt like hell nearly made me resort to tears. Ace was right. She doesn't want me, never did, never fucking will. She fucked up by messing with me. You can't go around breaking hearts and get away with it. When I love, I love hard and I think she took it for granted. She wasn't looking for love anyway. Too bad because it found her, and it's going to cost her, her life.

"I'll be back," I felt the urge to yell to Mel.

"Fuck you," she yelled back at me.

"Love you too."

The ice chill of November made my hand ache a little. I clutched it to my chest as I got in my car. I actually bought a ring for her. My plan was to propose on Christmas. It would have been our first Christmas together. Damn!

"Suckerrrrrrrrr," a voice whispered to me.

"Shut up," I snapped.

"What grown woman wants to play with a fun sized penis Brian?"

"Fuck you!" I snapped pounding my head to make them go away.

"She made a fool out of you Brian. What are you going to do about it?"

"Gut that bitch like a fucking fish."

*****

"What the fuck you mean he ain't here," I snapped. I paced back and forth unbothered by the deadly bite of the winter air. Montero my father's goon stood there looking at me with this blank ass stare on his face. "He didn't leave anything for me?"

"Not that I'm aware of sir."

"When did he say he would be back?"

"After the holiday's sir." I swear my heart dropped to my stomach. "When he comes back I will be sure to tell him that you stopped by sir."

"I'll be sure to tell him you stopped by sir," I mocked. "Get the fuck outta here. Fuck you," I snapped. His cool demeanor pissed me off. He didn't even flinch simply gave my crazy ass a nod.

I was so mad I couldn't think straight. I got in my car kicking up grass as I did three sixties in Big Brian's yard. Montero remained at his post as he watched me have a temper tantrum. I'm off my rocker and I know it but I can't get myself under control. I'm obsessed with finding Savannah and I won't stop until I find her and kill her. She did this too me. I was doing better, I was taking my medication, I was on top of my shit. And just like that she came in and fucked up my world. Well, I'm more than happy to return the favor.

Its well over two o'clock in the morning and sleep has forsaken me. My eyes are wide open, my mind is racing and I'm paranoid. I keep hearing shit, more than the usual. Somebody scratching at my damn door but when I open it, nobody's there. This is all Savannah's fault. If only she was a good girl, and loved me like I loved her I wouldn't be having these problems. I wouldn't be up two o'clock in the damn morning paranoid out of my damn mind. I'm restless and I'm getting the urge to do something.

My first thought was to dial her number but that would trace her back to me. I took a quick shower, and made sure I shaved all my body hair. Afterwards I dressed in all black, grabbed an old extension cord, a box of condoms and placed them in my back pack. I grabbed a bottle of wine then headed out the front door. I stood at the end of my driveway and staked out the neighborhood. It was still dark and quiet, the perfect night to do something and I'm about to do just that. I flexed my right hand. It still hurt at times but it was healing up nicely.

It didn't take me long to reach my destination. I knocked on her front door and patiently waited all the while looking over my shoulder to make sure the neighborhood was still asleep. A few minutes flew by and still no answer. I rubbed my hands together and knocked again. It was cold as fuck outside but the adrenaline that pumped through my veins kept my body warm. I wait a few minutes and still no answer. I turn around and survey the neighborhood before digging around in her flower pot for her spare key.

I don't know why people do shit like that. Honestly it's dumb. You never know who's watching and you're giving people access to your home. I insert the key, carefully unlocking the door and walked in. Its dark inside but I manage to adjust my eyes to the darkness. I've only been inside once and I'm trying to remember where her bedroom is as I make my way down the long hall. I pause in the living room to make sure everything is calm, it is.

Her bedroom door is unlocked. She's knocked out cold with one of those masks covering her eyes. She's sleeping peacefully, her chest slowly rising and falling. I stand there and watch her for a few minutes taking in her frame. Not bad at all. I know I said Halle Berry would be the only exception concerning age but Ms. Givens is an easy target. She's a lonely old woman married and divorced five times, with no kids, living off alimony. I need to scratch this itch that's been bothering me to do something bad. I continued to stare down at her because this is just too easy, besides I know she won't be missed. She begins to stir in her sleep and my dick pokes at my jeans. I guess she finally feels my presence because she jumps up and snatches the mask off. The look of terror in her eyes . . . priceless.

Savannah

"I didn't even know Savannah acted like that," my Aunt Tammy laughed as Brandon decided to take a trip down memory lane at my expense of course.

"Me neither. Matter of fact I think we were supposed to be on a break," Brandon said making air quotations. "But she comes up in the club acting all jealous. I think it was that liquid courage."

"Anyway can we move on please," I said rolling my eyes.

That night was so out of character for me. This little incident happened years ago. Brandon and I were on a break, my idea of course but I didn't expect to see him out with some chick a week later. This is one of the reasons why I don't drink or hang out at the clubs often because I somehow manage to make a fool out of myself. All I know is I had one to many shots and when I saw Brandon talking to some chick I lost it.

I waltzed my ass up there and made a damn scene. It got way out of hand and I ended up being escorted out. That was embarrassing. My mother was so disappointed and from that day forward I promised myself I would never allow myself to step out of character like that again. The situation could have escalated and cost me my future career as a nurse. I look back on it now and realize it just isn't worth it.

"So you just walked up on them talking about who is this bum bottom hoe bitch?" Aunt Tammy asked and cracked up laughing. "I'm sorry but I can't even imagine your proper ass putting the word hoe and bitch in the same sentence."

"This is a time of thanks and giving and we up here talking about stuff that happened years ago."

"That's what we're supposed to do right. Talk about old times," Aunt Tammy said rolling her eyes.

It's Thanksgiving Day. Were all here sitting at the table me, Brandon, Sabrina, Aunt Tammy and her new husband Ryan. So far things have been good, but I can't help but to miss my parents. This is the first Thanksgiving that I won't be able to share with them and it hurts like hell. I guess Aunt Tammy must have picked up on my somber mood earlier today because she came in my room and held me while I cried like a baby. What I would give to spend just another minute with them, even just to tell them I love them. I just wish I got the chance to say good bye.

"I know she just came over there like the matrix. I wasn't even doing nothing it was a girl I knew from school," Brandon laughed.

"Whatever," I said sticking my tongue out at him.

"Oh, since we are taking a trip down memory lane, did your aunt explain the story of how we officially met," Ryan said.

"Ryan!" Aunt Tammy started and Sabrina busted out laughing.

"No, go ahead," I said encouraging him.

"Well, me and a couple of guys were out at the bowling alley. You know just chilling. Your Aunt was there with a couple of her friends. Tammy caught my eye out the gate. She was the baddest one in the pack, but she was playing hard to get." I looked over at my aunt and she smiled. "You know I tried to get her number but she declined. My ego was bruised but I wasn't gone sweat it."

"So I guess Tammy tried to be cute when it was her time to bowl. She picks up a ball and tries to do this cute little run, making her ass jiggle a little bit. You know how women do when they know you looking," he said to Brandon. Brandon nodded his head yes.

"I was not," Aunt Tammy said rolling her eyes.

"Well, I don't know what the hell went wrong but she must have tripped over her own feet. She kind of did this little shuffle and the next thing I know was she sliding down the lane." We all busted out laughing except for my aunt. "She still held onto that ball though," he laughed shaking his head. "I ain't gone lie I laughed but I also went over there to help her up. Her wig had shifted; she lost an earring and a nail. So me being the gentleman that I am I retrieved her earring and that broken nail."

"This fool here was chuckling the whole damn time. He could have least made sure I was alright first," she snapped. She was trying to hold onto her own laughter but she couldn't. She had to laugh at the memory herself. "I was so embarrassed," she laughed, shaking her head.

"Were you trying to be cute mom?" Sabrina asked.

"Yeah I was."

"Did you hurt yourself?" I asked.

"Not really but my knee and thigh gave me hell the next day."

"So after I helped her up, and helped her fix her wig I made sure she made it to her car safe and sound. And that's how I got the digits, and she hasn't gotten rid of me since," Ryan said.

"I sure as hell tried."

"She did but I think I grew on her. It's my million dollar smile," he said stroking his chin. She rolled her eyes at him, and he leaned over and kissed her on the cheek. "I love you woman."

"Love you too man."

As I looked at them my heart got warm. I want that kind of love. I want that special someone who completes me. I looked at Brandon who was staring back at me. I guess he knew what I was thinking.

"Who's ready for some dessert?" Aunt Tammy asked.

"You know I am," Ryan said rubbing his stomach. He kind of reminded me of Nephew Tommy from the Steve Harvey Morning Show. I liked him. He's laid back and chill, a perfect fit for my aunt.

"Do you ladies mind helping me bring out the cakes and pies?" Aunt Tammy asked as she grabbed Ryan's plate and set it on top of her own.

"Sure," I said shrugging my shoulders standing up. "You finished with your plate?" I asked Brandon.

"Yeah," he said smacking my butt on the sly.

"Aight," I mouthed. I don't know what is going on with Brandon and I at this point. I know we need to talk. I know there are some things he wants to tell me and there's something I need to tell him. Apart of me would like to see where we could possibly take this. I mean the fact that he came all this way just for me has to count for something.

"Okay Sabrina can you grab the apple pie and the ice cream is in the fridge. Savannah you can grab the strawberry short cake and I'll get the sweet potato pie."

"Okay," I said eyeing the sweet potato pie she held in her hand. I loved my aunt's sweet potato pie and I couldn't wait to get a piece. I saved enough room in my stomach just for that. As soon as I picked up the strawberry cake, something about the strawberries made my stomach turn. The smell hit me and a wave of nausea washed over me. I put the cake down and made a bee line to the bathroom. I made it just within seconds before heaving everything I just ate into the toilet. I hate going through this again.

"Savannah are you okay?" my aunt asked before letting her self in.

"Yeah," I said nodding my head yes. She grabbed a wash cloth, wet it, and then handed it to me. I wiped my face and took a deep breath. My aunt looked at me with accusing eyes.

"What" I asked.

"So when do you plan on telling Brandon that your pregnant?" she asked. I sighed and shook my head.

"I don't know."

Roxie

I didn't think his old ass would be able to keep up with me but he had me fooled. I was doing all I could to pop this pussy and bring his ass to a nut, but I think he must have took a Viagra or something because it feels like we been going at it for hours and he ain't slowed down yet. He must not be getting it at home; either that or I got that snapper because he talking bout love already. I played into it because I need him so whipped that he'd be willing to do *anything* for me.

"Roxie, got damn," he screamed out as I placed my hands on his chest and placed my feet on the bed. I bounced up and down on his pole like my life depended on it. "Just like that," he breathed.

I rolled my eyes because I don't know what the hell he had for lunch today but his breath is sour. It smelled like stale chitlins. I almost lost my concentration the smell was so bad. Bad breath is a turn off and can fuck up ya sex life. I hope he is near a nut soon because I can't stomach much more of this shit.

"Oh, Papi," I whimpered into his ear as I continued to ride his dick.

He grabbed my hips and slammed me back down on his dick. I was getting frustrated. I was still wet but barely. The bad breath took me out of the game. I squeezed my pussy muscles tight holding his dick hostage as I picked up my pace. He squeezed my ass and I could tell by the look on his face he was about to tap out. He pulled me to him and sunk his teeth into my shoulder. He grunted a good four or five times before he finally released inside of me.

Finally, I thought to myself as I rolled over and snuggled up next to him. He placed his arms around me and kissed my forehead.

We lay there in silence for a few seconds. I knew he needed to catch his breath. I wanted him to marinate on the good sex we just had before I went in on him. I swear these niggas are so typical and predictable. Muthafuckas nowin days are so shallow all you need is a big butt and a smile. Glad I have both.

"Daddy," I cooed as I played with the hairs on his chest. I'm glad he couldn't' see the hard frown on my face. His body is repulsive. I mean flab every damn where. When you get older you don't have to let yourself go. I think that's why so many men go through these mid life crisis.

"Yes, Roxie," he said. I sat up so I could look at him. I gave him my million dollar smile.

"You know you got some good dick right?" I smiled. He blushed and that's just what I wanted to stroke his ego.

"Girl you something else," he smiled. That breath is horrible. My stomach turned and I almost lost my smile but I kept my composure.

"Only because of you daddy," I said licking my lips. I bet he was fine back in the day because he ain't hard on the eyes now it's just he got a huge ass gut. "Papi, what are we doing?"

"Cuddling."

"You know what I mean. I mean this kind of happened so fast. I can only imagine what you think of me," I said trying to give him my best sad face. I looked down before looking back at him. I conjured up some tears and rolled over on my side with my back facing him.

"Baby girl, what's wrong?" he said kissing my shoulder.

I started to tell him his breath is what's wrong. Got dayum can somebody say tic tac and pass this him about twenty of em. I ain't having any problems conjuring up some tears now, one whiff of that mess got my eyes all watery and shit. Vee just don't know the lengths I'm going through for her ass. This is all because of Brian's crazy ass that I'm even in this position. He wanted to be my best friend's man so he gone learn what happens when he fucks over a bitch like me.

I still can't believe he killed Mom Karen and Pop Gerald and to think that sorry ass Detective Harley is coming for me. That's okay because I got something for his ass too.

"Roxie!" Harold said kissing my shoulder.

You heard right, Harold. I'm bumping pelvises with Prince's dad and nope I don't feel bad about it. It's all apart of my plan. I can't wait until everything comes together so I can sit back and laugh at Brian's stupid ass. I knew Harold wanted me from the first day we met. He couldn't keep his eyes off of me. I played the victim after Prince and I broke up and it's no surprise we ended up in bed together. That's why I say fuck niggas, they just can't be trusted.

"I don't do this type of shit every day. This is new to me. I don't go around fucking father and son. This is going to take some getting used to," I sniffled.

"Take all the time you need baby," he said rubbing my back.

"What about your wife?" I asked him. I could feel the tension in his body as a deadly sigh breezed through his lips. I turned up my nose and rolled my eyes.

"Joan and I haven't been happy for years. All she cares about are those boys and spending my damn money. The only reason I keep her dry pussy ass around is because I didn't sign a damn pre nup. If I ever divorced her good for nothing ass she would get half of everything if not more."

So he's not happy with his marriage that's a bonus for me. I love when shit falls in place like I want it to. This should be easy, then again maybe not. Prince talked a good game but he had bitch running through his veins. If my powers of manipulation fail me I can always put shit in motion myself. I took a deep breath as I rolled over so that I was facing him. I gently caressed the side of his face.

"Well, if she doesn't know how to appreciate a good man . . . I do," I smiled. I kissed him and grabbed his package. I rubbed my clit and mentally prepared myself for round two.

*****

I was sore and worn out by the time I made it back home the next day. Harold old horny ass had me pinned up in every position imaginable. This was going to be a challenge but if I wanted to get some shit done then I knew I had to make some sacrifices. I needed a nice bath to wash away the icky feeling covering my body. I dropped my purse on my bed and stripped down to my birthday suit.

As my water ran I walked back into my bedroom and grabbed my phone. Nothing from Vee and that shit killed my spirit. Thanksgiving came and went and of course I spent it alone. I'm not usually the emotional type but Mom Karen, Pop Gerald and Vee was the only family I had. Now they're gone and Vee just up and left me. She didn't even have the decency to call me on Thanksgiving. She sent me a text. A fucking text like I'm some random chick she just met. Like we haven't been friends for over ten years. That shit cut me deep and hurt me to the core. I spent my Thanksgiving Day alone in bed all day crying. Just thinking about it had me in my feelings again.

After my bath I headed downstairs and decided on a bowl of ice cream. That's what I needed to cheer me up. I'd just sat down and got comfortable when there was a knock on my door. I glanced at the clock and frowned. It was a little after eight o'clock at night and I wasn't expecting any company. My heart skipped a beat at the possibility Vee finally returned. I sat my bowl of ice cream down and stood up smoothing out my lace nigh tie. I giggled as I jogged to the door.

"Who is it?" I smiled placing my hand on the door knob.

"Detective Harley."

"What the hell?" I said out loud snatching my hand away from the door. My eyes got lost in the back of my head and I sucked my teeth. I stomped my foot and folded my arms across my chest. "Can I help you?"

"I just have a couple of questions."

"At this time of night? Really?"

"It will take just a couple of minutes," he said. I still didn't budge. "I promise." I sucked my teeth.

"Hold on," I snapped. I ran upstairs threw on my robe and retrieved my Hermes bag before running back down stairs. I opened the door. Detective Harley still looked the same *dingy*. "What?" I asked not even bothering to hide my attitude.

"Can I come in?" he smirked. Imagine his surprise when I agreed.

"Sure," I smiled stepping aside. That smirk he had on his face left quick. "Well, are you coming in or not?"

He straightened up the jacket he had on. I'm sure it's seen better days. The smell of stale cigarettes nearly caused me to gag. I walked into the living room and sat down, before directing him to the lazy boy. He looked around skepticism all on his face before finally sitting down. I could tell he was put off by my sudden mood change. Now he was the nervous one and I liked it.

"Would you like something to drink?"

"Water would be fine," he responded. I didn't think he would say yes. But I sure did stick a finger in my ass and stirred it around in his water.

"Here you go," I said handing him his glass. His ungrateful ass didn't even say thank you just took the glass and started drinking. I rolled my eyes on the sly than sat down. "So what brings you here at this time of night? Kind of late don't you think? People might get suspicious."

"Don't flatter yourself sweet heart." He had the nerve to chuckle.

"I know . . . I'm not your *type*."

"Lets' cut the bull shit. You know why I'm here. I know you killed Gabrielle Leah. Make it easy on yourself and confess."

"Oh Detective Harley if you know I killed Gabby why haven't you arrested me yet? Seriously! What's up with all the accusations? Do you have any proof of such nonsense? You keep harassing me and I just might have to file a law suit."

"Somebody saw the two of you together early that morning. Said you were walking together hand in hand. You had on a gray sweat suit and a pair of white tennis shoes."

My jaw literally dropped but I quickly picked it back up. I didn't want to give away that I was guilty but it was too late. He knew from the beginning, but I wasn't worried because he really doesn't have any proof but he does have a witness. Somebody out there know's my secret.

"Where is this so called witness then? Why haven't I been arrested?"

"Just confess Roxie. You were a minor at the time and from what I can see you've kept your nose clean. I'm sure the DA will make a deal. Manslaughter, you'll serve fifteen years the max."

I looked at him like he was crazy. I couldn't contain myself as I burst out laughing. He was seriously out of his mind if he thought I was spending time in any body's jail. I would die first. I couldn't see myself being locked up like a caged animal.

"Why does this case matter so much to you? What the fuck is in it for you anyway?" I snapped, but he skipped over my question.

"You haven't even denied the accusation Roxie."

"So," I said shrugging my shoulders. "You don't have shit on me because if you did I'd be in jail by now."

"I'm trying to help you Roxie," he said doing his best to sound like he really gave a damn about me, but I watch Investigation Discovery. Those pig muthafuckas will try to play the sympathy card quick like they have your best interest at heart. All they looking to do is put another notch on their belt and I'd be damned if I fall for the ole okie doke today.

"Detective Harley both you and I know that you are full of shit. You're only doing this for your career."

"Roxie-,"

"I'm tired Detective Harley," I yawned and stood up. "I think this conversation is over."

"Bitch," he mumbled under his breath.

He is really in his feelings about this. His rude ass brushed passed me purposely bumping into my shoulder. It took everything within me not to clock his ass upside the head but I held my cool. I grabbed the pictures out of my Hermes bag and followed his scent to the door.

"Detective Harley," I called out as soon as he stepped outside on the porch. "This is the last time we speak. Make it go away or else," I snapped throwing the pictures I held in my hand in his face before slamming the door. "It's good to know people," I said out loud to myself.

I waltzed my happy ass back to the living room. He must have gotten the message because he actually left peacefully. I grabbed my cell phone and sent Bri a text message. I'm lonely and need to release some tension. I ain't gay but Bri got a sick tongue game. She'll have a bitch climbing the walls and shit. I glanced at the clock it's only a little after nine.

Me: What's up Boo?

Bri: Hey chicka nothing much bout to head to crazy eights in a few. Why what's up?

Me: I'm horny

Bri: Sorry chilling with bae tonight.

I frowned and dialed her number.

"Hello," she answered loudly smacking her gum in my ear.

"Whose bae?"

"You know."

"Oh so you choosing Ace over me huh?" I asked faking like I was mad.

"I can come see you tomorrow Roxie. I'm about my money bitch just like you."

"If that's the case why Ace still got you shaking ya ass down at Crazy Eights?" I asked throwing a little shade. "But anywhoo did you ever find your house key?"

"Nope," she said sucking her teeth. "Glad I have a spare."

"You think Prince might have taken it?"

"Nah, I don't think so. I'm sure he would have used it by now. If he does use it he will be highly disappointed, because bae sure will be waiting on me. Prince talks a lot of shit about Ace but I know he don't want them problems."

"Have you talked to him lately?"

"Nope and I ain't checking for him either."

"You really feeling Ace ain't you?"

"Yeah," she sighed. "But I know that nigga ain't looking for love. But I'm riding this ship until it sinks."

"Aight chick I won't hold you up. So you stopping by tomorrow night then?"

"Yeah, I'll be over later."

"Smooches," I said hanging up.

I jumped up from the couch and paced my living room floor. Nervous butterflies took refuge in my stomach. I breathed deep. I had to get myself together. I glanced at the clock it was going on ten so that didn't give me much time to do what I needed to do but it's crunch time. It's either now or never.

Detective Harley

My hands trembled as I stared down at the pictures that bitch Roxie threw in my face. I've kept this double life secret for years, but this bitch manages to get her hands on some confidential information. I grabbed my bottle of cognac sitting in the passenger seat and took a long hard swig. I gagged a little and pounded at my chest.

I ripped the pictures in half and stared off into space. My life is shit. My marriage is over and my career is in the dumps. I haven't solved a case in years. This latest scandal could ruin whatever dignity I have left.

I needed this case. It was a cold case ruled an accidental drowning. At the time I was just a rookie getting my feet wet. No one believed me when I pointed out the facts. Her clothes were ripped and the pond wasn't that deep. I got an anonymous phone call about a week later telling me they saw Roxie and Gabby walking together hand in hand early that morning. I tried to get the caller to come forward and make a statement but they refused. In the beginning I never suspected Roxie. I was just pulling her card but the look on her face said it all. .. She's guilty. This would have revived my career or at least I hoped. After years of being a lead detective I know it's my time to retire but I can't. It's all I have.

I took another swig of my cognac as I grabbed my wallet. I put my bottle down temporarily and pulled out the old picture I kept of my wife and two boys when they were younger. They are all grown up now working on families of their own. We don't talk much. I can't blame them. I wasn't much of a father. I put my career, and lover before them.

My lover, my life, my secret . . . I'm gay. I've fought this battle for years. I knew the moment me and my child hood best friend acted on our sexual impulses at the age of fifteen. We loved each other but there was no way could be together. Society frowned upon homosexual activity. I wanted to follow in my father's foot steps and become a police officer. If I came out of the closet I knew no one would ever take me seriously.

So I ended my relationship which eventually cost me my friendship as well. I was at the top of my class in the academy. After three years on the force I met my wife. She'd just graduated from college with a degree in nursing. She was a devout Christian and made me wait until we were married to have sex. I didn't mind because my heart lied else where but for the sake of appearances I had to do it. I love my wife, she's a good woman I'm just not in love with her. Despite my distance and lack of affection she has stayed by my side.

Five years into my marriage my best friend, the man that held my heart came back into my life. Like me he was married with two daughters. He's an attorney and had success on Maryland's Western shore but he said he couldn't stay away no matter how hard he tried. We've been going strong since. But lately because of the downfall of my career I haven't been spending much time with him. Not like I use to.

Besides he complains about my appearance. Always nagging me about shaving, wearing the same clothes three days straight and I just don't care anymore. I've given up. The thought of my secret getting out has finally pushed me to a breaking point. I take another long swig of my cognac. I grabbed my phone and decide to send my wife a text.

Me: Please forgive me for not being a good husband and father. Thank you for all of your love and support although I didn't deserve it. I love you.

After I hit the send button I turned my phone off. I grabbed the pictures, a lighter and my gun. I got out of my car, but quickly ducked back inside the car and retrieved my bottle of cognac. I walked down to the pond. The same pond Gabby was drowned in. I took the pictures of me and my lover in compromising positions and set them on fire. I watched the pictures become engulfed in flames while I finished my bottle of cognac, threw the bottle in the water, placed the gun to my head and pulled the trigger.

Brian

This muthafucka finally decides to call and says he has the information. Mind you he called me around twelve this afternoon but he said I couldn't pick up the information until ten o'clock tonight because he had business to handle. That's my father's way of controlling me. I'm pissed but there ain't much I can do about it. I need his ass cause he sure don't need me.

Time ain't moving fast enough for me. I'm anxious as hell to find out where Savannah is so I can wring her fucking neck. That bitch played me like a fiddle and my dumb ass let her. Damn if only I listened to Ace from the beginning. But she fucked up when she took my number and called me. If she didn't have any intentions of being in a relationship then she should have lost my damn number, but she chose to play with my emotions instead. Now I'm hell bent on making her regret the day she decided to start fucking with me. I'm itching to tell her ass it was me who killed her parents. Imagining the look on her face has my dick nearly standing at attention.

I grabbed my boxing gloves and took my frustrations out on the speed bag. Every blow I threw I imagined it was Savannah's face. I hate when a bitch plays with my time, my money, my heart. Then she decides to up and leave without even so much as a kiss my ass. That was childish. She should have been a woman about hers. The outcome would still be the same but I could at least respect her a little more. I went another thirty minutes until my hand started hurting.

I walked to the kitchen grabbed a bottle of water then headed upstairs to my bedroom. I threw my gloves on the bed, stripped out of my workout gear and headed to my bathroom to take a quick shower. When I walked back into the bedroom my phone was ringing. I glanced at the caller ID, it was Ace. I feel bad for leaving everything in his hands. I know he probably still in his feelings about putting the opening of the club in Miami on hold. I can't blame him but I was in a fucked up state of mind but once I handle this situation with Savannah then its back to business.

"What's up Big Bro."

"You tell me."

"Nothing really just got a little work out in. How them numbers looking?" I asked sitting down on my bed.

"Must be nice to take a vacation after a vacation."

"Here we go," I sighed. I can't even argue with him because in a way he has a point. We did business down in Miami but we had some fun too, well I attempted to. Melinda did all she could to keep my mind occupied but nothing worked. Not even her head game.

"I'm just saying."

"So you called me just to be a bitch."

"Yep."

"Look I know I've been slacking and haven't been pulling my weight but that's what we got Mace for to look after shit also. I'm dealing wit some things right now but it will be handled soon and after that I'm back in business."

"I love you Brian but I swear you have got to be one of the dumbest muthafucka's I know. You got all this going for you and sittin' here ready to throw it all away over some bitch."

"You'll never understand Ace."

"You damn right I won't. I don't want to either. Just walk away Brian." After a moment of silence I gave him the answer he was looking for.

"Aight," I sighed. He sucked his teeth.

"You're just saying that. You don't mean that shit, I know you B."

"No, you're right, Ace. I haven't been pulling my weight and I've let this Savannah shit get to me. I just took a shower I'll be there just give me a minute," I said as I rubbed my hand over my head.

"That's cool. I won't be there anyway. It's Thursday, that's usually one of our slow nights. It's only nine thirty so it's a nice little crowd but not the usual Friday and Saturday crowd."

"Wait, you just getting on me about taking a vacation, where the fuck you at?" I asked heading to my dresser and grabbing a pair of sweat pants. I didn't realize it was this late. He laughed.

"I'm ready meet up with my bitch. I swear her head game so good it'll make a nigga toes lock. The way I've been working I deserve a break sheit."

"Got dayum," I chuckled. "Tell her get at ya boy."

"You crazy, but I gotchu. She a freak. That bitch tried to lick my ass though. I ain't down wit that gay shit. I smacked the hell out of her ass for that one."

I laughed but I've let a couple of bitches toss my salad, a few niggas too for that matter. I don't see anything gay about it as along as a I ain't penetrating or being penetrated. Say what the fuck you want, but I would never tell Ace no shit like that though. He already looks at me funny as it is.

"It is gay Brian," a voice said in my head. I take a deep breath and ignore it.

"I feel you on that big bro. I bet she tried to kiss yo' ass afterwards too.," I laughed.

"Hell no. I don't kiss none of these bitches in the mouth. That's too intimate and I don't need them to get the wrong idea. We just straight fucking I don't need them to start catching feelings. We just fucking, hope these bitches know don't come looking for love. That's how you gotta do it B. I ain't looking for nothing serious right now, I got too much I'm trying t build. Once I'm established I'll be on the look out for the right one but until then I'm just having fun."

"Yeah you right," I said nodding my head in agreement. By now I'm fully dressed, with my keys in hand heading out the door. "Well, I'm on my way to the club. Have fun and strap up," I said lying through my teeth. I really had no plans of making it to the club tonight. I just wanted to give Ace peace of mind.

"Always."

Forty-five minutes later I was at my father's house. As always I had to go through the same ritual but I'm use to it by now. When I got to my father's office he was sitting behind his desk with his bright ass robe on and a cigar hanging from his mouth. He didn't look his normal self though.

"What's up Pop," I said sitting in the chair across from him. He coughed and grabbed his left arm. "You aight?" I asked.

"Yeah," he frowned rubbing his chest. "She's down in Savannah Georgia. Her aunt just remarried and relocated to another part of Georgia with her husband. Savannah's down there with them. The address is in that envelope," he said pointing to the white envelope laying on his desk with Savannah's name on it.

"Thanks Dad," I said as I anxiously stood up and grabbed it. Yes, finally. I'm glad I finally got her location just mad I had to go through all this for an address. "Well, I'll let you get back to whatever you doing. I'll holla."

"Brian-"my father croaked. I looked up just as he grabbed his chest. "Help me," he said reaching out to me before stumbling to the floor.

"Dad," I squinted as I walked around to the side of the desk where he lay on the floor. He had his arms stretched out to me but I didn't budge just stood over him. I smiled at his agony thinking my prayers have finally been answered. I leaned over and whispered in his ear. "See you in hell muthafucka."

I threw up a pair of deuces as I walked out of my father's office. As I was leaving I bumped into Montero.

"Hey man I just want to apologize for the way I acted the other night. I'd been drinking and smoking a little too much weed."

"It's all good no hard feelings. I'm on my way to see your father now. He wasn't looking all that good earlier. I wanna make sure he's straight. That's my bread and butter."

Not anymore, I thought to myself.

"I feel you, but he looked fine to me. I don't think he wants to be bothered though. He was on the phone and he seemed upset. He needs to leave them cigars alone," I laughed. He laughed too.

"Aight, I'll get up with him later then. I don't want him going off on me. You know ya Pops got a few screws loose. No offense."

"None taken. You have a good night," I said patting him on the back.

"You do the same."

I glanced at the address I held in my hand. The smart thing to do would be to wait until she comes back. I know my father's death is going to spark some attention but I can't let her get away that easy. Rest won't come until she's dead, and I every intention of making that happen.

Bri

"Come on ma just one hour of your time is all I'm asking for."

I rolled my eyes at this lame. He trying to get fucked and sucked for fifty dollars. Please you can barely get a decent meal for fifty dollars. Hell that chump change can't even fill up my gas tank. Besides I got a big juicy dick waiting on me at home and I ain't fucking that up for nobody.

"Not tonight, I'm busy," I said as I brushed past him to make my exit.

"Man fuck you then bitch." I shook my head. Typical insecure nigga can't handle rejection.

"Nope, you can't afford to fuck wit a bitch like me. Fifty dollars really?"

I glanced over my shoulder and laughed at his pathetic ass. Even if he was □alking' real money I wouldn't fuck with his dusty looking ass anyway. I turned my nose up at his dark complexion and pink spotted lips. That's when I spotted Meesha walking in his direction. I knew she would take him up on his offer. She's a thirsty bitch. She'd fuck on GP for a pack of cigarettes and a dime bag of weed.

I miss life on the Western Shore. The niggas over there had so much more to offer than these broke bums around here. Working at Crazy Eights is aight but it ain't shit compared to the money I made in B More. I sigh and try not to think about my current situation. I plan on returning this summer, just maybe in a different area. This time I'm going to snag me a rich eligible bachelor. I'm getting to old to be fucking around wit another bitches man. Besides too many disease roaming around out there for me to keep up with that lifestyle.

I kinda miss Prince a little. He didn't mind stacking a bitch with some bread, but he wasn't on boss status like Ace. I don't know what it is about that dude it's just something about him that keeps my panties wet. As much I would like it to, I know me and

Ace really isn't going anywhere but I can't help my addiction to him. It has to be the sex, and the money because he shows me no kind of affection. No kissing on the lips, he barely gives me fore play. I mean he plays in the kitty and might suck on a titty here and there but that's about it. He's never even attempted to see what she smells like although I'm on all fours every time we get together.

Sighs!

I walk outside and wrap my coat tighter around my body. It's cold as hell and I feel every bit of the November weather gripping my bones. The parking lot is nearly empty with the exception of a few fake ballers still hoping to cash in on some action. I threw them all kinds of shade as they attempt to get my attention.

I jogged to my car nearly tripping in my stiletto's but I made it safe and sound. You can't trust nobody now in days. Niggas be waiting for bitch to slip up. But I make sure to check my rear view mirror constantly. I don't need nobody looking for a come up off me. Forty minutes later I pulled up to my house. Ace is already here because is Lexus is parked in my spot. I suck my teeth and roll my eyes as I step out.

It's my fault because I put up with him. You ever have a nigga whose dick game so sick he'll make you do stupid shit. Stupid shit like he has a key to my house and I ain't even stepped foot in his. Never seen it, never been invited, nothing. Straight stupid shit like leaving every body I done fucked with alone just so my pussy will be on call whenever he in the mood to fuck. I did it though. I missed out on some good money fucking around with his ass.

As soon as I stepped foot inside I slipped out of my heels. I bent over and rubbed my feet before standing up to stretch. I stood in the hall way listening. Something didn't feel right and all of a sudden I felt sick to my stomach. Chills rolled off my spine and I stood there in silence.

"Ace." I called out as I headed upstairs to my bedroom. I figured that's where he probably was. I didn't hear the television playing downstairs so more than likely he was upstairs. "Ace," I yelled out again.

It felt like it took me forever to reach my bedroom. I don't know why the hell I knocked but I did. After standing there for a few minutes I didn't receive an answer. I turned the knob and pushed the door open. I flicked the switch and screamed at the top of my lungs.

"Fuck! Shit!" I scream as my eyes frantically look from side to side.

There was so much blood. My bladder folded as I ran downstairs. I fumbled with my phone dropping it in the process. It crashed to the floor and fell apart but I couldn't bring myself to stop and pick up the pieces to put it back together. I ran to my next door neighbor's house and banged on the door, but no one answered. I can't blame them. I know it had to be about two or three o'clock in the morning.

I can barely see as I ran across the street because my eyes are full of tears. I run up the steps to Mr. Marcus house. I drop to my knees as I bang on his door. I didn't even realize he opened the door.

"Bri," he said looking around outside.

"He killed him," I whimpered.

"Who killed who?" he asked as he helped me to my feet and walked me inside.

I was too distraught to answer. He kept asking me the same question I couldn't respond. I cried my heart out until the police finally arrived.

Prince

"Excuse me," Yasmine giggled looking back at me like that shit was funny.

I can't believe this bitch just farted while we're having sex. I turned my nose up, and my dick instantly deflated. I pulled out and headed to the bathroom and closed the door.

"I said excuse me," she snapped like that would make it better. Yeah right.

She ain't all that anyway, just something to pass the time by. She and I went to high school together. We fucked around from time to time, it was never anything serious. Back then she was the school hoe, it was easy pussy. Ain't shit changed since then except she's gotten a little thicker. I mean she got a fat ass, just a whole lot of stomach to go with it. She cute but she ain't Bri or Roxie status. Damn I done fell off a little bit but I'm gone bounce back.

Bri fucked with my heart heavy. I thought I was in love with Roxie, but Bri had my ass gone. It wasn't just the sex either. Bri and I could sit and have actual conversations. She was like my homie lover friend. Unlike Roxie who only acted like she was interested in the fact I had dreams. That bitch got a few screws loose anyway. I can't believe she almost talked me into setting my brother up, shit is crazy.

I grab a wash cloth, wet it and then wipe my piece off, then headed back out to my bedroom. Yasmine grilled me as I walked back out but I shrugged it off. Her pussy was whack anyway, my shit couldn't even stay hard because her walls are so dry. I glanced at the clock it was going on five o'clock in the morning. She's over stayed her welcome, it was time for her to bounce.

"Aight I'm a get up wit you later. I'm getting ready to go to bed."

"What?"

"I said I will get up wit you later I'm getting ready to go to bed."

"So what you saying I can't stay here?" she asked with an attitude.

I breathed hard and ran my hands down the side of my face. I couldn't blame nobody but myself for the madness, but she was getting the hell up out of here. I 'm not in the mood to entertain her ass. I licked my lips and nodded my head yes.

"For a lack of better words that's exactly what I'm saying. I'll get up wit you later."

"Man fuck you then. Soft dick muthafucka, you can't fuck worth shit anyway," she snapped as she rolled off the bed and began to collect her clothes. I almost lost my appetite at the sight of her stomach. It looked like a fucking grilled chicken with the black lines running across it. I guess she caught the look on my face. "What the fuck you looking at me like that for? You ain't mind when you was digging up in these guts," she snapped as she bent over and snatched her purse off the floor. "Can't even keep a stiff dick. My time and pussy is valuable."

"Bitch get the fuck outta here with that shit. Who could stay hard pussy smell like old chicken grease. I only fucked wit ya ass cause I felt sorry for you and it was easy pussy, but I didn't think I would have to work this hard just to get a nut. Good pussy, bitch fuck you and that stale dry ass pussy."

"Fuck you," she screamed as she opened my bedroom door.

"Nope that dry duck you got between ya legs wouldn't even let me do that right. Bring some Vaseline next time so I can lubricate them walls."

I laughed to myself as I followed her ratchet ass downstairs. I can't believe this bitch tried to come at me like that. She got a fat ass though. I watched it shake as she stomped down the hall way. As soon as she opened the door a gun was pointed in her face.

"Ahhh," she jumped back.

"Get on the ground now?" two uniformed police officers barked while pointing the gun in my direction. Yasmine didn't have to be told twice. She literally fell to the ground. I put my hands in the air.

"What the fuck is going on?" I frowned.

"Sir, I need you to slowly put your hands behind your head and get down on the floor." I nod my head and do as I'm told. He walks up to me followed by several other police officers. He places a knee in my back as he grabs my wrist and proceeds to put me in handcuffs.

"Yo' what the fuck is going on?" I asked again. I can hear my heart beating in my chest.

"Are you Princeton Lewis?" he asked ignoring my question.

"Yeah, that's me. What did I do? Why am I being arrested?" Just as soon as the words left my mouth a uniformed officer walks in holding a plastic bag.

"I think we found something," he said before looking down at me. I watch as he pulls out an old shirt of mine soiled in blood. "I think this may also be the murder weapon," he said holding up a long butcher knife with the tip of his finger. My heart sank because I knew where I'd seen that knife before. The officer who put the hand cuffs on me looks down at me and smiles.

"You're under arrest for the murder of Acello Davis."

Roxie

I hummed and smile to myself as I poured antifreeze into Joan's tea. I know she will be flying in soon once she hears the news about her precious Prince. Harold just doesn't care. He got me all up in his house with no shame, sleeping in his wife's bed. She still on vacation and to be honest I don' t think she is the least bit worried about his ass. He said he only heard from her twice. I stirred up Joan's tea and placed it back on the shelf. I closed the refrigerator and nearly jump out of my damn skin. I swear this chick has no shame. She getting real bold, just popping up in people houses like this.

"Gabby what the hell do you want?" I snapped, looking over my shoulder as I quickly walk past her and put the bottle of antifreeze back in the garage. I took the gloves I had on off and put them in my back pocket. She shakes her head and folds her arms across her chest.

"This is so sad and pathetic, but then again I wouldn't expect anything less from a sad and pathetic soul like you," she said. I frown.

"What?"

"Come on Roxie. Who put's all this time and energy into ruining other people's lives? That's sad don't you think?"

I rolled my eyes. I wonder to myself how the hell is she talking like this and she's only ten but then I realize she's just my conscious talking. I don't even acknowledge her just keep on walking. Maybe if I continue to ignore her ass she will get the hint and finally stay away.

"Savannah's going to find out. She's going to find out everything. About me, about Brandon and the baby, and once she does you are going to lose the one person you worked so hard to keep her."

That got under my skin a little. I whipped around to address her but she was gone. I breathed deep and wiped the sweat off my lip. I headed back upstairs. When I walked into the bedroom Harold is just getting off the phone. He has a strange look on his face. I sit down on the bed beside him and rub his back. "What's wrong baby?" I ask although I have a slight idea why he looks so upset. He sighs and rubs his chin. I get a whiff of his breath and I almost throw up.

"It's Prince. He's in jail."

I do all I can to keep in what I felt on the inside from coming to the surface. Everything is falling into place just like I hoped. Killing Ace was easier than I thought it would be. I was the one who stole Bri's house key. When I called her the other night and she spilled the beans about Ace being at her house I knew it was fate. I knew I had to act quick, so I put on one of Prince's shirts, a pair of his jeans and tennis shoes that I held onto just for this purpose and left my car in a local park not to far from her house.

I used her key and let myself in. It was quiet as hell and at first I didn't think he was there but then I remembered seeing his car parked in the driveway. I quietly walk upstairs and that's where I found him, in her bedroom passed out. I slit his throat from ear to ear before he knew what hit him. I wasn't expecting all that blood though. It was every damn where, and so was he flopping around like a damn fish. I wonder what he was thinking when he took his last breath. Anyway once he finally stopped fighting the inevitable I dipped my finger in his blood and wrote Prince's name on the head board. After that it was smooth sailing. I placed the clothes and knife in Prince's trash can and called Harold up for a night cap establishing my alibi.

"Roxie did you hear what I just said?" Harold asked me interrupting my thoughts. I shake my head.

"I'm sorry baby. Jail?" I asked faking like I was shocked. "What's he doing in jail? What did he do?"

"Murder?" he said rubbing his head.

"Oh my gosh," I said placing my hands to my mouth. "That doesn't sound like Prince at all," I whined as I rubbed his leg. "It will be okay baby. Do you want me to go down there with you?" He shook his head no. "I understand just know that I'm here for you. I'm sure there has to be some kind of mistake."

"I hope so," he sighed. I continued to rub his leg, before making my way up to his inner thigh. I felt the tip of his dick peeping through the tip of his boxers. I looked up at him and smiled. He had that look in his eyes despite the fact his son just told him he was in jail.

"So are you trying to go down there now or what?" I asked reaching inside of his boxers stroking his man hood to life. He licked his lips and closed his eyes as a slight moan breezed through his lips.

"He can wait."

That's all I needed to hear. I didn't hesitate to drop on all fours and place all nine plus inches he had available in my mouth. This is like taking candy from a baby.

Savannah

Loving you is really all that's on my mind. And I can't help but to think about it day and night. I wanna make that body rock, sit back and watch. Tonight I'm gonna dance for you (ohh ooh ohh ohhh). Tonight I'm gonna dance for you (ohh ooh ohh ohhh). Tonight I'm gonna put my body on your body Boy I like it when you watch me, ah. Tonight it's going down. I'll be rockin' on my babe rockin' on my babe. Swirlin' on my babe. Twirlin' twirlin' on my babe. Baby lemme put my body on your body promise not to tell nobody cause it's about to go down.

The look in Brandon's eyes had my pussy soak and wet. I stayed in sync with Beyonce' as I dropped down to the floor into a split. He's leaving tomorrow so I figured I would leave him with a little something to remember. He's been dropping hints since he been here. So I did it for old time's sake. I'm rocking lingerie underneath a white button up. No heels though I'm not that good I ain't trying to fall and bust my ass.

"Pop it! Pop it! Pop it for you baby!," I sang along with Beyonce' as I popped my ass on Brandon's crotch. I smiled to myself because I feel the imprint of his dick. I still got it.

He didn't even let me finish dancing. He picked me up and lay me down on the bed. He growled into my ear as he lightly bit my shoulder. I rolled over on my back and wrapped my arms around his neck. He groped my breast as he inserted his tongue into my mouth. He pressed himself against me and I opened my legs so he could feel the heat in between my thighs.

He ripped my shirt open, took off my lingerie before taking a detour down south. I bit my bottom lip and moaned his name as he devoured my clit into his mouth. He placed two fingers inside of my love box stroking me to a climax.

"Fuck!" I cried. I felt my juices as they squirted into his mouth. "Brandon!" I whined as I attempted to push his head away.

"What's my name," he came up briefly before diving back in head first.

"Daddy," I cried as I lay back down and enjoyed another tongue lashing. I lifted my hips off the bed as he bought another orgasm out of me. He smacked my ass and before I could blink he was in me. He stroked this pussy so good I fell asleep.

*****

"Savannah!"

I yawned followed by a stretch. I open my eyes to find Brandon looking at me, slightly stroking the side of my face. Something is wrong I can see it in his eyes.

"What's wrong?" I asked. He sighs then he leans down to kiss me. He kisses me aggressively and with so much passion it scares me. When he pulls away from me I see the tears in his eyes. "Brandon, what's wrong? Talk to me." He takes my hand and kisses the back of it.

"We need to talk."

"Okay about."

"Do you remember when I cheated on you?" he asked. I frown.

"Brandon why are you bringing this up now? It's in the past and I've moved on from it. Let it go."

"I can't. You need to know the full story," he said sadly. I wiped away the tears that have fallen from his eyes. "Savannah I cheated on you with Ro-,"

Loud banging coming from downstairs stopped him in mid sentence. It was so loud it caused me to jump.

"Who the hell is that?" Brandon said out loud.

"I don't know," I said sitting up and grabbing my robe from off the back of my bedroom door before heading downstairs. The banging was so loud it reminded me of the night my parents died. "Who is it?"

"Brian!"

"Who?" I asked. My heart literally dropped to my stomach.

"Savannah open the got damn door," he snapped. Against my better judgment I did. I open the door and peeked over my shoulder to make sure Brandon hadn't followed me. That's all I would need for him to bring his big yellow ass down here and it would definitely be World War III up in here. "Brian what the hell are you doing here?" I asked looking him up and down. He looked tired. This is kind of scary. I wonder how the hell did he find me?

"So this how you do me Savannah? Got me all over creation searching for your ass."

"Brandon, I -,"

"Brandon! Do I look anything like that yellow big bird looking muthafucka," he snapped as he pushed his way inside.

"Look I know your upset and I'm sorry I left the way I did. But if you're going to act like this I'm going to have to ask you to leave."

"Savannah!" I heard Brandon call my name.

"Fuck!" I said dragging my hands down the side of my face. I should have never opened the damn door. I'm praying it doesn't come back to bite me in the ass.

"Savannah you good?" Brandon asked.

"Yes, just give me a minute please." He nodded his head yes and I directed my attention back to Brian.

"So this is how you do me huh? Play with my emotions. If you didn't want me Savannah all you had to do is say it instead of being a bitch about it and jumping ship. What grown ass woman does shit like that?" he snapped.

"Hey don't-." Brandon started but I held my hand up and shook my head no, then I turn back to Brian.

I frown and give him a side ways glance. We've already established our relationship status but now he coming at me like I left without giving him an explanation. Crazy! This is what I get for trying to be nice, well I'm tired of being nice. I ain't sugar coating it no more. I ran my tongue over my teeth and fold my arms across my chest. I'm going to say it so he finally gets it.

"Brian, it's over."

He smiled as he closed the door behind him. "Baby girl it ain't over yet. We're just getting started."

The tension was thick. I looked back at Brandon. I felt a sense of relief he was here. I don't know what the hell I was thinking answering the door for Brian's crazy ass anyway. I wondered how he found me. I will figure all that out later. I need to figure out a way to get him out of here and quick. All I need is for Aunt Tammy to come home and make a scene.

"Brian, you need to leave," I said wrapping my robe tighter around my body and folding my arms across my chest. He had the nerve to smile. I use to find that smile charming but now it's just creeping me out.

"Like I said before Savannah we're just getting started so I ain't going no where," he snapped. He had the look of death in his eyes.

"Yo' did you hear what she said?" Brandon barked. I snapped my head around and looked at Brandon. I shook my head no. I didn't want things to escalate. Brian looked like he was off his rocker. "Savannah!" Brandon screamed as he started towards me. The look on his face caused my heart to skip a beat.

I turned just in time to see Brian holding a gun in his hand and it was trained on Brandon so I reacted. I grabbed Brian by the arm and elbowed him as hard as I could in the stomach. It did the trick because he went stumbling backwards but not before he let a shot off. He still had a tight grip on the gun so I sunk my teeth into his wrist. I was in survival mode. I had an unborn child I was determined to meet. I wanted my second chance at happiness. Through all the commotion I didn't even have time to think about Brandon. I was just trying to get the gun away from Brian's crazy ass.

"Bitch," he hollered out in pain. He let off another round before finally dropping the gun. He grabbed the back of my hair and pulled. I screamed. It felt like he was trying to rip it from my scalp. We fell to the floor and he still had a hold of my hair. I felt him reaching for my throat so I jabbed my finger in his eye. "Fuck," he screamed finally letting go of my hair.

I scrambled to get off him as I looked around for the gun. It was on the floor beside his foot. I grabbed it and quickly stood to my feet. I kept the gun trained on him doing all I can to keep my hand from shaking. I hear Brandon in the back of me moaning and groaning. I look over my shoulder and he's on his back holding his chest. A puddle of blood is starting to form around him.

"Brandon," I shouted as I willed my feet to move and back peddled towards him.

"You really gone shoot me Savannah," Brian began to taunt me. "Do it!" he said sitting up.

"Don't move," I said through gritted teeth. My heart is racing and my bladder has reached it's full potential.

"I hope that muthafucka choke on his own blood," Brian snapped as he chucked spit out the side of his mouth. He glared up at me. "This is all your fault Savannah. You should have never played with my heart. You led me on. Made me fall for your sorry ass all the while you fucking the next nigga."

I didn't dignify that with a response but kept the gun trained on him as I kneeled down beside Brandon. His shirt is soaked in blood and my heart broke. Brian is right this is my fault. I never really wanted Brian, I just needed something to pass the time by, now Brandon is paying for it.

"Its not as bad as it looks," Brandon said. "He just got me in the shoulder," he said grimacing in pain. I remained silent because he had two bullet holes not one. He was leaking from his chest but I didn't say anything.

"Here hold this," I said quickly handing him the gun. I took the belt from my robe and made a tourniquet near the wound. Then I used my robe to apply pressure to the wound on his chest. It was soaked with his blood within seconds. That scared me.I took the cell phone off his hip.

"Before you do that Savannah, I have to tell you something," Brian said now sitting with his knees propped up and his elbows resting on his knees. Blood dripped from his wrist where I bit him. "I . . . killed . . . your . . . parents"

"911 what is your emergency?"

I couldn't even find the words to say anything. They were lodged in my throat because I was stuck in time. I slowly stood up as I removed the phone from my ear. It fell to the floor.

"Savannah," Brandon said tugging on my arm.

"What did you say?" I said in a voice barely above a whisper.

"I killed your parents," Brian laughed. He threw his head back like he actually said something funny. I shook my head from side to side as the tears continued to roll of my cheeks. "Yes," he laughed as he nodded his head yes. "I did. I had too-,"

I didn't give him a chance to finish. I grabbed the gun from Brandon and took a few steps forward.

Boc!

Boc!

After the second shot I went numb. I kept firing, even after the clip was empty.

"Savannah," Brandon whispered grabbing my arm.

I dropped down to the floor and screamed at the top of my lungs. My parents are dead and it's all my fault.

To be continued ...
Look me up on Facebook
Author P Dotson

Made in the USA
Middletown, DE
13 November 2018